AN ILIA ARCHIVES NOVELLA

SILVERWEAVER

CAMERON MONTAGUE TAYLOR

First ebook edition October 2023 | First paperback edition October 2023

Ebook ISBN: 979-8-9889069-0-2
Print ISBN: 979-8-9889069-1-9

To the meow who read it,
the red who listens to my brain soup,
and the soups who always make sure I'm telling
the stories I set out to tell.

This little novella isn't what I'd call dark, but to make sure we're on the same page, *Silverweaver* contains violence, fraught familial relationships, possession, body horror, and spooky creatures doing spooky things.

One

"Oh, come on, Taran—it's one measly ghost. What's the worst that can happen?"

Taran avoided meeting my eyes, turning his scowl instead on the book of matches pinched between his fingers. "I'm not getting mixed up in your hunting," he said, then picked a match to strike and dropped it into the gas lamp on the rickety table between us.

The lamp illuminated the dreary break room he'd corralled me into, sending shadows skittering up its bare walls. Calling it a "room" was a bit generous, to be fair, because I stood elbow-to-elbow with stock shelves and an overburdened garment rack, the latter of which had some rich ponce's greatcoat hanging from its hooks. It belonged to Taran's boss, no doubt. Saints knew my brother wasn't rolling in silvermarks from part-time work as an old-city guide.

"I'm not getting you 'mixed up' in anything," I said. "It's a single night of working together on one of your tours, just to see how you like it."

"This is my *job*, Anya." He folded his arms and leveled me with *the look*—the one he'd inherited from our mother. It sent his brows crawling up his forehead to an upswept widow's peak of dingy dark hair. Not that I'd point out it could use a washing. He'd have a fit—as if medical students didn't forget to feed themselves without reminding. "If something goes wrong, my boss will—"

"I'm a professional. Whatever happens, I can handle it, all right? And, look, if a ghost shows up on your 'low-season discount special,' think about the tips you'll get."

Taran's lips pressed into a thin line, but his eyes darted from me to the open break room door, then back to me. He was going to say yes; I could feel it. No one recognized performative indecision better than a ghost hunter.

But his next words weren't the emphatic agreement I'd hoped for.

"I've heard stories, all right? About hunters who come up to businesses and ask to do *this exact thing*, then stir up a whole host of trouble." He picked at the midnight-blue cuffs of his coat, the uniform of Ilia's most prestigious university. "I never thought you were one of them."

My hackles rose, shoulders jumping to my ears. "Hey. I'm not some two-bit fraud. I can't believe you'd—"

Taran turned away, striding across the room to close the office's iron-fitted double doors.

He could have shut them without moving—wrenched them off their hinges, even. So could I. Metalweaving ran in our family, and we were a proud bunch for it—artisans, merchants, architects. Taran took after our mother and studied medicine. Enough iron ran through blood for skilled metalweavers to manipulate it, placing us among Ilia's finest trauma medics, but I suspected Taran was headed for surgery. That'd make our parents proudest. Prouder than I had made them, at least, though that wouldn't take much.

Apparently, it's a disappointment when one of your seven kids runs off to become a ghost hunter.

That was how my mother framed it, of course, but I never *went* anywhere. I completed an apprenticeship with an Ilian hunter, struck out on my own when my contract was through, and paid most months' rent without scrounging for low-level jobs.

Besides, I dropped out of medical school ten years ago. My mother should have forgiven me by now, and one would think *Taran* had no reason to care, since he was nine at the time. Alas, that wasn't the case.

"I'm under no obligation to put myself at risk to support your lifestyle," Taran said once the second latch clicked, words taken straight from my mother's mouth.

They thought ghost hunting was a dangerous waste of potential. Maybe it was, but I did it for the love of it, something they'd never understand.

I had one issue with my work: seasonality. Ghosts liked the summer months—only the Saints knew why—and stayed away from Ilia's spiritual epicenters for the rest of the year. The only credible winter work came with the rings. They won the big contracts every hunter wanted, ones that paid a stipend to keep them on retainer for protecting the old buildings in the city center.

And that protection was necessary. Unlike their gentle counterparts, malignant spirits had no compunctions about showing up in the colder months. When they did, ghost hunters had to act quickly or risk horrific consequences. It wouldn't surprise me if Taran had read last week's headlines. A spirit went dark-side on the fringes of the old city, killing three people before the hunters showed up.

There was a reason those contracts took a lot of clout to get. Alas, clout was the one thing I didn't have.

"We aren't talking about the same thing," I said, pushing the words through grit teeth. "The hunters you're on about are the scum of the industry. They stir up malignant spirits or try to get benign spirits to go dark-side. Then, when they banish them across the veil, they charge a protection fee. You lose your ghost, *and* you get robbed blind. That's not me, all right? I'd come back home with my tail between my legs long before I started provoking spirits for cash."

And if hard times ever forced professional dishonesty on me, I'd never expect Taran to enable it. Tour guiding paid his school bills. Just because I didn't want to follow in our mother's footsteps didn't mean I wasn't proud of him and his choices.

Moreover, I'd never put him—and the people on his tour—in danger just to make a mark.

"Somehow, I doubt that," he muttered, fiddling with his neckerchief. "All right, fine. Let's hear your plan." As if he could smell my incredulity from across the room, he added, "My lab fees are piling up. I could ask Mom for money, but you know how that is. I've seen some of the other guides walk away with massive tips after taking ghost hunters on their tours—"

"So, you want in." I cracked my knuckles, unable to stifle my tiger's smile.

Taran's sigh was so dramatic it ruffled the sweep of hair on his forehead. "I want to know what it's going to cost me."

"Nothing. Hunter's honor." I made the sign of the Saints over the lapel of my leather coat, a tatty brown thing that had nothing in common with Taran's fancy blues. "I find a sleeping spirit. I nudge it awake. The dullards on your tour get to ask it the same set of questions they all ask ghosts—*when did you die? Why are you here?*—and I put it back to sleep again. Easy as falling off a log, and we'll walk away with a week's worth of silvermarks for an evening's work." I flicked my plait over my shoulder, a dark whip that rested halfway down my back. "Come on. What have you got to lose?"

"My job. My self-respect," Taran muttered. He scrubbed a hand down his face. "All right. I need those marks. But if you tell Mom about this—"

As if I'd ever.

I snorted. "I don't have a death wish."

His twisting mouth betrayed how unsavory he found the deal, but I didn't rise to the bait, holding out a fist for him to clasp.

"All right, Yaya," he said, using my old nickname from his nursery days. I hadn't heard it in years. "Don't make me regret this." He wrapped his hand around my fist and squeezed.

Yes. Taran was far too much of a stick-in-the-mud to go back on his word. "I'll see you tomorrow at the old church. Sundown. Tell your clients it'll be the best midwinter's tour of their lives."

The doors opened with a sweep of my hand, and I strode through them, past the lobby, and out into the frosty Ilian morning.

TWO

MY HIRED CARRIAGE CLACKED through the narrow streets of Ilia's city center, bouncing me across the backseat. Iron-reinforced wheels were a nice touch for metalweaving drivers but horrible for a passenger's comfort—especially when the driver had a thirst for speed. I braced all four limbs like a nervous spider, wincing when we took a snappy turn and teetered onto two wheels. This was the hidden cost of booking a discount ride with a university kid. What I saved in marks, I paid in years shaved off my life.

Saints, after all the malignant spirits I'd banished, it'd be fantastic irony if a ride did me in.

We careened past a flock of pedestrians, tilting another precarious inch. That was enough for me, and I wove out from my gut, reaching for the iron spinning in the carriage's lifted wheels. One push, and they slapped back to the cobbles. The driver turned to glare at me through the screen, but my expression must have warned her against mouthing off about my interference.

Honestly. Her driving was appalling. She was lucky I'd always been too much of a bleeding heart to stiff another weaver on a tip.

The carriage skidded to a stop at the southern gate of the old city's ruins. I flipped a silvermark from my pocket to the screen and held it there, suspended with a thread of power, and opened the door. It let out a tooth-rattling squeak as I hopped to the street.

"Should get some grease on those hinges," I said, releasing my thread when hers brushed the coin.

A metalweaver's handshake.

Freed from that death-trap, I popped the kinks in my back and surveyed my surroundings. The street's verve outstripped its cramped confines. My sister's spinning metal installations—the pride of the art institute—studded each plaza. Paintings by waterweavers ran along the sidewalks. One beneath my feet depicted a school of rainbow-hued fish, colors fading with twilight's advent. Animated by rainfall, they'd swim through the street at the first touch of water. Winter's dry bluster froze them still.

Shadows cast by Ilia's spindly towers fell across the entrance to the old city, and I crossed beneath its wrought-iron gates with a prayer to the Saints on my lips. A shiver raised baby hairs on the back of my neck. Spirits slept through the winter, sure, but they did so on this side of the veil, and even a second-rate ghost hunter with no gift for spiritweaving could sense their presence.

Some spirits remained behind for years without crossing. They made their home here, and Ilians tended it with care. Weavers called it the spirit-city, Ilia's heart, an enclave of ancient, empty buildings. The living ringed its edges and only passed through for visits, for prayer, or for little tours like the ones Taran guided. The dead gave us the same courtesy in return. In the summer months, they'd wander up to the central district but wouldn't stay past nightfall.

Easy harmony until one of them went dark-side.

Whipping wind blew dead leaves in miniature cyclones, turning past cracked stone facades. The old city had presence, had weight, like an iron yoke on my shoulders. I tugged my coat tight. *Saints*, it was cold, and my family's southern blood couldn't withstand an Ilian winter. I'd rather be sitting in a tavern in central watching a fireweaver spin, but Taran wasn't the only one pressed for marks.

If I didn't suffer the cold now, I'd suffer it when my overdue rent came back to bite me.

Taran was with his tour group, huddled outside the church, chattering in friendly anticipation. Most of them hailed from cities to the north—the only explanation for their disinterest in layers and furs. They'd tease us while we shivered, calling Ilia's bluster balmy.

The church they'd chosen was an ancient thing. Stories-high with knife-point peaks, its towers thrust at the sky in a wild appeal to gods Ilia no longer believed in. Though guides kept the grounds tidy, they went to great pains to preserve the *ambiance*, and the open door revealed an interior boasting cobwebs and dusty furnishings. Nothing had changed since the last time I took a winter contract. How long ago was it? Three years? Four? It would have been with Eleira. *El.*

I rubbed my breastbone with my knuckles, willing the ache away.

El was a spiritweaver, a ghost hunter so talented she was hunted in turn—by wealthy families, foreign institutions, big-city types who prized her skill and discretion. She'd left Ilia for greener pastures at the first opportunity. It cut more than I'd ever admit.

Not that I thought, even for a moment, she'd stay in the city for my sake. Trust a heart not to listen. It broke when she left, anyway.

With a flutter of blinks, I cleared my vision. No time for wallowing. I had marks to make.

I put my mind to business and patted at my coat, triple-checking my tools: a set of daggers, vials of salt, incense, and two books of matches wrapped in wax cloth for waterproofing. Taran looked up when I approached, hair flopping from its fashionable sculpture as it caught the wind. I opened my mouth to heckle him but froze when I noticed the man standing at his shoulder.

The newcomer had a northerner's pallor, with high cheekbones and wheaten hair. We were of an age, I figured, but that's where the similarities ended. He had the sort of handsome face and affable aura that made fast friends and inspired trust—or so I thought—until he spoke.

"That's not even a spiritweaver." His eyes fell to my boots and climbed up again in a look that mimicked the many university professors who'd assessed my work and found it wanting.

I wasn't unused to fielding unfavorable judgments—plenty of Ilians prized spiritweavers over their elemental brethren—but it got me heated every time.

My hands disappeared into my sleeves, fingernails carving half-moons into my palms. "I'm also not a cat, a biscuit, or a fishmonger. Now, if we're done making a list of things that aren't relevant—"

"When I heard there was a hunter on the tour, I assumed I'd be working with someone competent, not a . . . whatever you are."

He said it as though I should have slapped my magemark on my coat, like my mother did with her workwear. As if pride made a weaving talent. He had no leg to stand on, for his jacket was the same tatty brown as mine: no fur trim, no quilting, nothing to mark him as a member of a first-rate family. This was my least favorite type of client, one who lorded his scrap of superiority over me at every opportunity.

I opened my mouth to tell him to shut his, only for the full weight of his words to register.

"*Working with*," he'd said.

His coat was plain, but it had the telltale signs of professional modification. Double-breasted. Deep pockets. An extra-high collar. He wore it open, and a silver-handled dagger glinted on his hip.

My head snapped around, and I fixed Taran with my best *big-sister glare*, his stupid pride be damned. "You brought another hunter on your tour?"

"Lower your voice, Anya." He tugged me away by the elbow, prodding me down the steps until we walked among a row of decrepit churchyard shrubs. "The tour is overbooked. We've got two guides and almost thirty clients. If you're doing a summons—or whatever you call it—I don't want to take any risks."

My face was on fire. "*Risks*?" I hissed. "You think trusting me to do my job is a *risk*?"

"You're not a spiritweaver. If you're going to hunt on this tour, I want backup. Calix is backup."

That *idiot*. He'd talked Taran into this—of that, I had no doubt.

"You've made tonight a lot more complicated and a lot less profitable."

"Have I? Anya, I know you." Taran's nostrils flared, eyes like chipped marble. "When you don't like the way things are going, you disappear. Why should I trust you not to vanish on me if this goes bad?"

His words hit like a slap. As he designed them to, no doubt. "Are you seriously *still* talking about me dropping out and leaving the house—"

"And what else have you stuck with since then?"

My mouth opened. Shut. *Hunting, obviously*, I wanted to say, but he wouldn't agree. Taran counted success the university way, and unless I stacked up on his measuring stick, my work meant nothing.

Taran's grip on my elbow eased. "You're almost thirty, and what do you have to show for it? No medical degree, no professional contract, no family—"

"*Saints*, again with the reminders—what are you, our mother?"

Whatever piece-of-work reply Taran had saved up was cut blessedly short by a shuffle behind us, followed by someone calling Taran's name.

I spun to find the group on the church steps had doubled in size. At their base was another tour guide. She had a shock of white hair, wore a blue university coat, and approached with a gaggle of clients at her heels. A woman in brown walked at her side.

I knew that face.

Heat drained from my cheeks. My stomach somersaulted like an overzealous street performer.

The tour guide's lips moved, but I didn't hear a word of it, attention fixed on a different kind of ghost—a living ghost, one I'd seen in dreams for years and would know with my eyes shut and a bag over my head.

Eleira Soti was back in Ilia.

THREE

El's face struck me like a spear through the heart, and the only thing I could summon was a hollow laugh. As always, my mouth moved without my say-so. A predictable inanity tumbled out.

"Well, well, if it isn't Quicksilver Soti here to show Ilia how it's done."

I cringed when the words hit my ears. Dull as usual—bitter, too—and not at all what I meant. Certainly not how I'd imagined a reunion with El going when I let myself indulge in daydreams. It wasn't the welcome she deserved. I held out my hand, hoping she'd ignore my running mouth.

Bless her, she didn't even notice, launching herself my way with arms out.

"*Spirits*, Anya!"

A bounding leap, and she was there. Without thinking, I dropped my cheek onto her shoulder and squeezed tight. My teeth ground, eyes leaking. She smelled the same. Like daring hunts, like home, like incense and lavender soap. I clutched her, relearning how *right* she felt, with a waist made for my arms to wrap around and a body built stronger than an iron gate.

She pulled away to get a look at me. Losing those inches hit like a bucket of ice water. "I tried to find you, but you've moved, and I didn't have time . . ."

El was brightness and sunshine, a warm spot on a horrid, cold evening. Ruddy-cheeked, she wore a silly woolen hat, out of which an auburn braid hung to the center of her back. Flyaways framed her face. Her necktie was a mess. She was gorgeous. Still. Always. In every way possible—the kind of weaver who ghostly spirits loved for her heart. A hunter who'd lay me out in a spar and apologize for it afterward, rueful, as though it was her fault I didn't block a punch.

My throat rebelled. My mouth filled with lead. My hands shook for wanting to reach up and touch that face with its blade-edged jaw, its button nose, its smile that infected anyone who saw it.

"What are you doing here?"

Saints, what was wrong with me?

"Oh." El stepped back, smile falling. Cold air snaked between us. "I'm so sorry—if I'd realized the tour company contracted, I never would have suggested it, but Piri is a friend of the family, and I thought I'd help her with her tips—"

The light-haired tour guide offered an awkward wave.

Great.

"I—I'm not working with a ring." I stepped aside. "We had the same idea. Scare up some tips. You know how it is."

Only then did El notice Taran, a valley of confusion furrowing her brow.

Once upon a time, El and I won contracts that tided us through the winter. Small but steady ones. Anyone who knew Ilian hunting said we were headed for good things, like an invitation to join a ring in central. Vanguard, maybe—or, in our wildest dreams, Silvershield. After she left, it turned out there wasn't much work for a lone metalweaving ghost hunter.

For El to see firsthand how far I'd fallen, that I'd stooped to begging my kid brother to bring me along on his old-city tours? I'd hoped she'd *never* find out.

El opened her mouth, then shut it. "Is it . . . a bad winter, or?"

I couldn't meet her eyes.

"It's been a bad few years, though that's more of a 'me' problem than an 'Ilia's ghost population' problem." I sensed the question forming on the tip of her tongue but wanted none of it and turned away. With a bright clap, I brought her eye to the dunderhead standing at Taran's side. "Anyway, seeing as how there are three of us hunters—Calix, El, El, Calix—we'll get a nice show together for these fine folk. Isn't that right? Taran, why don't you and Piri lead the way?"

Calix had not a word of doubt for Eleira Soti, famed Ilian spiritweaver. He fell into line with mouth shut and hands deep in his pockets.

If my absolute wreck of an evening was obvious to Taran's clients, they didn't let it show. They gathered around their guides on the church steps, and an expectant hush rippled through them as the tour began. I wiggled into the middle of the crowd, focus trained on Taran and Piri, and pretended to pay attention to a rundown of facts I could recite in my sleep.

Built over a thousand years earlier out of hand-hewn granite blocks, the church was presumably the work of early stoneweavers who didn't yet understand the full extent of their powers. It stood much as it did back then, undisturbed in recent centuries, ever since the first spiritweavers began speaking to the dead. We called those weavers the Saints—the only word we had for them at the time—but the moniker wasn't inapt. They'd saved Ilia and her surrounding cities by guiding the glut of lost souls through the veil. Without them, the violence plaguing city centers would have gotten worse until it drove us from our homes to start anew.

Instead, the Saints paved the way for the sanctification of the old city. Spiritweavers, all, they shook off the yoke of false gods and ushered in a new age of peace.

We metalweavers had our patron saints of a sort, too—Jalti the Stronghand, who bent the copper flashing from Ilia's tallest tower into a pike and slew an enemy general with it in the eighth century. Lotha Baili, the inventor who tuned the gears in automated clocks. Osrin Aglaia, the first doctor to cure demonic blood poisoning. No Ilian would argue against our utility. But spiritweavers?

They were essential.

I shuffled toward the vestibule with the group and watched them *ooh* and *ah* their way up the center aisle to the altar. Dust-coated pews lay in rows on either side. Taran and Piri lit the space with gas lamps, though the faintest blue light still filtered through stained glass windows, tinting furnishings in frosty tones.

The light reflected off relics in the church proper, setting the space aglow. Holy metal. Scavengers had stripped some in the years after the old city's abandonment, but most of it remained intact: great candelabras and overhead lanterns, filigree, embossed frescoes. Everything silver. Mythology was rife with it in the old days—and for good reason. It *worked*. Iron formed barriers for spirits, but to banish anything, hunters used silver. It was the one skill metalweavers had over our spiritweaving counterparts.

The silver tickled at the edges of my senses, warm and alive and full of potential. Was this why Taran chose tour guiding over other work? Surely, he felt it, too. Surely, he saw—if only the littlest bit—why I liked hunting so much. Whose heart wouldn't be moved to wonder by a city of ghosts and memories?

Yet, the church wasn't as I remembered it. It was winter, sure, and most of the ghosts were absent and resting. But something *not-quite-right* needled me—

Footsteps.

El appeared behind me, fingers worrying at the wool cap she'd doffed. "Anya, listen—"

"It's fine."

What was fine? I didn't know. But I sensed the arrival of a conversation I'd long dreaded and had no desire to have it. Not now.

"I'm sorry," she said. "I didn't mean to single you out on the steps—"

I snorted. "If you think that got to me, you should hear how well Taran parrots my mother these days."

The consternation etched into El's face didn't ease.

"I thought . . . well. I assumed you'd have a contract by now. A big one, with one of the rings, or maybe—"

My bark of laughter earned impatient shushes from the group and a dirty look from Taran.

I dropped my voice to a whisper. "What, you think a ring like Silvershield—home to the city's most talented—would hire a solo metalweaver? Oh, that's rich."

"A weaver like you? Of course." She wore an expression I couldn't examine too closely lest my heart beat hard enough to crack my ribs. "You're better than this."

What would she know? She *left*.

I huffed, quieter this time to avoid drawing Taran's ire. "Not all of us can get headhunted by the big city."

El opened her mouth to argue, but Taran finished his speech and announced my name with an expectant stare, the same one he used to wear when begging me to take him to the park as a kid for weaving practice. I wasn't around much back then. My nails dug into my palms, banishing the guilty trickle of memories.

I had work to do—work for which both Calix and El were blissfully silent as I cleared the center aisle and lit a stick of incense. It'd take a minute for the scent to permeate the room and call to the spirits who enjoyed it. They'd rouse partway, and the three of us could nudge them, see if any were feeling chatty that evening.

But even as the incense wafted thick in the air, something felt *off*. The church had a strange presence within its walls, one that made it difficult to connect with the sleepers. I brushed my uneasiness aside. It was midwinter. Resting spirits often needed an extra push to wake them this time of year.

Unfortunately, the best push I'd ever found was my own singing. At least my inability to carry a tune never seemed to bother them. El once told me it was a matter of kind intentions. I disagreed. No being, living or dead, slept through my rendition of "Round Goes the Daisy."

Clearing my throat, I edged to the door for a better view of the pews where the tour group gathered. A briefing on the next step was due, not only to review ghost protocol but also to warn them about the forthcoming lullabies. For a province filled with cities built to accommodate spirits and their needs, most were stunningly ignorant of how hunters operated. I didn't mind teaching them. It was fun to be a part of someone's first summoning.

The crowd's eyes fell on me, drilling holes in my skin. I cleared my throat again. It was time to show them what I was best at, Taran's doubts be damned—

A familiar *unfamiliar* shiver ripped up my spine. I froze. Something was here.

No. *How?* I hadn't called. The church held no restless spirits—I was sure of it. But whatever rose came too quick, too soon, raking my senses as though it was already awake. I should have noticed it the moment we walked in. El should have heard its call.

And, oh, whatever it was, it was *angry*.

A man cried out, pointing to the altar, where it poured from ceremonial silken screens with a vengeance. Frosting stained glass windows, it whipped down the aisle in a fury, guttering our gas lamps.

I spun. Behind me, El reached for the dagger at her hip. In two steps, I stood at her side, falling into place with shoulders together. No time to look for Calix. A dark shape formed in the archway to the vestibule, smoke billowing out from the ether.

"What in Jalti's name is *that*?"

I forced the words through grit teeth, but El didn't reply, dagger raised and brow etched with concentration. I wanted to throw an arm in front of her, to tell her to stop and not to open her mind to it. This was no friendly ghost nudged awake by a nursery rhyme. But what was it? I hadn't started the summons—let alone finished it—and even if I had, I wouldn't have ended up with *this* for my efforts.

A chill prickled at my nape, standing my hair on end. It was growing, *expanding*. My head snapped around as it reached for the ceiling.

"Oh, this is *not* good," El muttered, digging through a pocket.

Saints, let her have salt spray—we'd need it.

On either side of the aisle, Taran's clients cowered in the pews, whispering. A kid started crying. His parents hushed him, and his wails faded to soft sniffles.

Someone gripped my shoulder—Taran. It didn't take a heartweaving talent to notice the cloud of fury on his brow.

"Anya," he hissed, "that's no benign spirit."

The moment the words left his mouth, every window in the church shattered.

FOUR

Glass waterfalled into the altar room. A downdraft of cold air followed, whether from Ilia's winds or the spirit's interference, I couldn't tell. I'd flinched and ducked as the windows shattered, throwing an instinctive arm across El's back, but sprang to stand when the spirit whipped away to block the door. It gathered there, a whirling, hesitating mass, as though it took stock of the church and hunted its next target.

I tossed my stick of incense and ground it beneath a boot. No time to waste. This spirit woke on the wrong side of the bed, and I'd be piked by Jalti before I let it take a hit at the tour group. My silver knife leaped into my hand, drawing the spirit's focus like a magnet, and I dropped my shoulder and charged.

El fell in at my side as an arm of black smoke unfurled from the doorway. I pushed her out of the way just in time. The spirit pricked my skin with phantom needles, hissing when I raised my knife. Yet, it didn't flee with the urgency I'd expected, retreating instead in a raking glide, each movement tugging at my senses.

My eyes lost their focus. A dark drumbeat thrummed in my ears. I leaned in, taking a step forward once, then again, then—

A hand closed around my arm and yanked me back. Something snapped in the air, as though a string connecting me to the door had parted. My head cleared. I raised my knife again, and the spirit thickened, shrinking and compacting. For a moment, I swore I stared into a pair of bottomless black eyes—

And then it was gone.

A breath skipped out of my body.

What. Was *that*.

To hide the tremor in my hands, I fussed with sheathing my knife, then turned my attention to the group in the pews. They huddled, a mass of pale faces and whispered prayers, but none appeared injured. The glass shower hadn't reached the seats beside the center aisle. *Thank the Saints*. Taran never would have forgiven me.

I'd never have forgiven myself.

"Anya. What did you *do*?"

I'd given thought to Taran's forgiveness too soon, it seemed. He'd recovered from his shock and stalked up the aisle, the very picture of our mother in his outrage. As tempted as I was to take offense at his lack of faith, he wasn't a hunter. He couldn't know I'd never finished the summons.

"Nothing, and that's the problem." I took two steps and retrieved my incense, then tucked it into a pocket. "I didn't call *that*, whatever it was."

When I turned, I found Calix at Taran's side, looking down his nose at me yet again.

"That spirit is either malignant or on the cusp," he said. "Something must have startled it. Or should I say . . . *someone*?"

Imply I'd bungled the job, did he? Misdirection at its finest. Taran, alas, didn't know the difference.

"You're going to have to send it across the veil, and when my boss hears about it, he will *skin me.*" Taran threw up his hands. "This is going to cost me my job. I can't believe you—"

I grabbed him by the elbow and dropped my voice. "I need you to listen carefully. Whatever that was, it wasn't part of anyone's plan. That makes it dangerous. If we're going to fix this, I need you to trust me—"

"Why should I?" He pulled his arm from my grip. "You ruin everything."

He didn't mean it—not the way it sounded. He was angry at me for leaving, for spending so much time away, for loving a job he couldn't or wouldn't understand. But Taran had a way of running his mouth and hitting where it hurt, of turning his own heart outward and making a weapon of it, and *Saints* if it didn't sting.

I turned away, striding up the aisle for the altar. It was that or blow my temper in front of El, Calix, and thirty clients.

He wasn't entirely wrong, either, which was the worst part. I'd never excelled at the things our family cared about. Now he'd walk away from the old city thinking I was a bum hunter, too.

What Taran didn't understand was how many ways there were to wake a ghost. Beyond that, they just *appeared* sometimes, hence the need for low-season contracts. And that—a rare, spontaneous appearance—was my top theory.

El had stood in my sights the whole time. And Calix? He'd been behind me, but I'd have heard his incantations for a summons. None of us had spoken. The church's newest addition must have awoken before we arrived. It was the only explanation. Yet, the answer wasn't comforting in the slightest, for never in my years on the job had I seen a spirit—even a malignant one—react to incense like *that.*

El followed me to the altar in a patter of footsteps, catching me when I hit the first platform. "Anya? *Anya*. Wait. Try not to take it so hard? It was uncalled for, but he's always been tetchy, and believe me, I know you're not a bumbler. That wasn't you."

If anyone had my measure, it was El. She'd seen me hunt more than anyone.

I spun, searching her face for any sign of doubt, but found none. "What was it, then?"

"Maybe high season is coming early this year."

A ridiculous platitude.

"Even if that's somehow the miraculous case, we still have *that thing* on our hands and a church full of frightened northerners."

I needled her out of habit, an impulse I couldn't help, while inwardly praying she'd have an answer. Could I chase the spirit down with a silver knife and a handful of incantations? Sure, but it wasn't liable to end well.

"I have a plan."

I resisted the urge to sigh with relief. Of course she did. El always had a plan, always knew the next step.

Saints, I'd missed her.

As we spoke, Calix left Taran's side and joined us on the altar. He'd caught the tail end of El's words but didn't challenge her, waiting instead with arms crossed and brows raised—the very picture of imperious impatience.

But El was unflappable, as always. Her eyes slid shut, and though I wasn't a spiritweaver, I knew she used her talent. A breath slipped past her lips, long and slow. Whatever she sought she must have found, for her nose wrinkled, and her brow furrowed in a little crease.

I loved that face. Scrunched-up focus. Tongue poking out the corner of her mouth.

"It's attracted to the altar," she said, springing into a flurry of motion—a pint-sized whirling dervish of activity, casing the lay of dusty relics with the frenetic interest of a cat burglar. "I can't tell why, but that's not unusual. Spirits attach to objects. We caught it off guard, and now, it's agitated. This is where it wants to be. It's not happy we're here, though, so helping it cross will be a challenge."

Calix tracked her progress back and forth across the altar. "We'll keep the tour group seated in the pews. It'll come straight up the aisle—"

"Are you daft?" I stabbed a finger at what was left of the windows. "After what we saw, you want to bring it into a room full of people? No. We get them out of here first."

He huffed. "Attempting to leave will draw its eye to the vestibule. I wouldn't expect you to understand much about spirits, but . . ."

I'd fling him ass over teakettle if there weren't witnesses. *Saints*, I'd do it anyway if one of them wasn't *Taran*, who nodded along with everything coming out of Calix's mouth, as if he knew a seance from a summons.

"I'm steering us clear of collateral damage," I said.

"And how do you propose we do that, metalweaver? You think it'll let us walk away?"

He wasn't wrong. If the spirit was fully dark-side, it wouldn't let us out to the street without a fight. Not if it had us where it wanted us. I'd gotten into this hoping to make a mark, but silver lost its shine when I considered what might happen if we tried to guide thirty civilians past a malignant entity with the power to shatter that many windows.

I needed El's help. El's *and* Calix's, as much as I hated to admit it.

When I turned to El, I found her already looking at me, as if waiting for me to give her the go-ahead nod. Old habits. As soon as I did, she launched into the plan she'd cooked while Calix and I sniped at one another. By the time she was halfway through, we started completing one another's sentences.

"It might just work," she said. "If we position ourselves in the vestibule—"

"At cardinal directions, with the door at the fourth—"

"With incense, incense will distract it—"

"Taran and Piri can guide the others out—"

"It won't follow them, would it?"

"Nah, it'll come for us, especially if we turn for—"

"The altar, as I said. It's attracted to this place. We'll send it across from here and lay it to rest. Peacefully." El beamed at me, color high in her cheeks.

She practically vibrated with the excitement of a well-laid plan, and I couldn't help the grin I shot her in return.

Calix cleared his throat. "Incense?" His brows arched. "Because that worked earlier? Are you both in the habit of bringing spoons to knife fights?"

I hesitated.

Incense attracted and pacified spirits, but something about the way this one had reacted to it stuck in my craw. Yet, if the alternative were salt . . .

"I'm not salting a spirit until I'm certain it's irredeemable." El folded her arms. "It's inhumane, and I can't believe you, as a spiritweaver, would suggest it." She pointed to the doorway, finger shaking with gorgeous, righteous fury. "That was a person once. A father, a daughter, a child. I'll be burned before I wipe them from existence without doing my diligence. It's against everything we were ever taught." Her eyes flashed. "Unless you know something we don't?"

Calix's jaw ticked. "Only that I don't like putting people at risk."

He'd raised his voice when he spoke, making sure he was loud enough for the group to hear him.

They murmured at his words, eyes falling on El as though she was the risk, the renegade, the problem.

Absolutely not.

"Listen, *hunter*," I said, jabbing the center of his chest with my finger. "El Soti is one of the finest weavers in the business. If you're going to work with us, I suggest you fall in line. Otherwise, you can find your own way out of this church."

He opened his mouth but decided against whatever idiot thing he was about to say, and shut it with a click of his teeth.

I caught El's grin out of the corner of my eye, which was bright enough to light up the cobwebby corners of my chest. Great. Less than an hour after running into her on the church steps, I was back to working with Eleira Soti. *Mooning* over Eleira Soti.

As if no time had passed at all.

El held her fist out Calix's way. "Are you with us?"

He hesitated, gaze flicking to the doorway where the spirit had stood. "I don't like this," he said but relented, wrapping his hand around hers. "But, yes, I am. For now."

"Anya?"

"Where else would I be?"

If I thought she'd flashed me a grin before, the response I got for *that* was blinding, chasing the last icy echo of the spirit's shadow from my skin.

"All right," El said, cracking her knuckles. "Let's get them out of here."

Five

"Incense?"

"Got it."

"Matches?"

"A whole book."

"Knives?"

I rolled my eyes. "What am I, a rookie? Of *course* I have knives."

"You know me and my ounce of prevention," El said, grinning. She bounded by, passing Taran and Piri on her way up the aisle, straightening the tour group's formation.

The tourists glommed together in the center aisle. Though the broken windows had stunned them to panicked silence, several had recovered their wits and demanded information—or, in one case, a refund.

The matriarch of a northern family took her grievances straight to the guides, interrupting Piri mid-sentence with a browbeating that would have put my mother to shame. Taran, all too accustomed to filial warfare, slunk off and left her to take the brunt of it. I had no compunctions about thwapping him in the back of the head on my way to rescue her. I certainly didn't stay to listen to his affronted griping afterward.

As it turned out, however, Piri didn't require rescuing. Calix reached the head of the column before she melted beneath the matriarch's onslaught, his easy manner and charming grin brighter than an open flame.

"It's all right," he said to Piri. "These things happen—especially in the old city." Addressing the woman, he added, "I'm terribly sorry for the inconvenience. But rest assured, we'll get the spirit back to where it belongs, and when we do? You won't want to miss it."

His words comforted Piri, but they didn't reassure me. "You won't want to miss it" was the kind of sideshow talk hunters used when they were aiming for tips on a slow night. Sure, I'd had marks on my mind when we met on the cathedral steps, but now, they were the least of my worries.

From the back of the column, El and Taran flashed us a *ready* sign. El had the bright-eyed look of a hunter on the job. Taran, less so. He wound the edges of his cuffs tight around his wrists, then unwound them, then wound them again. When he was a kid, he fussed with his nightshirts the same way, always after running into my room and begging me to banish the monsters under his bed.

Now, instead of fictional monsters, we faced off against the real kind. I could forgive him for his snit. Taran never had much love lost for the things he didn't understand.

Heaving a big breath, I returned El's *ready* sign, spun on my heel, and slapped Calix on the shoulder on my way out the door.

My stick of incense lay in my palm, but I kept it unlit while I moved through the vestibule to get a feel for the space. Laid out like an upright cross, a pair of dark halls sprang to the left and right of the door to the church proper, and a fountain of still water stood between them. It broke direct access to the exit, but past it, the vestibule opened up enough to hold the tour group in its entirety. *Perfect.*

The exit lay on the far side. Night had fallen, and the distant glow of streetlights beckoned. Ilia's steady wind blew dead leaves in to patter across marble tile. It swept around my shoulders, ruffling the flyaways escaping my braid—my only company. The spirit was gone.

I stuck my head back into the altar room, where Calix and Piri stood. "Ready?"

Piri nodded, drawing herself tall. "Quickly, now," she said to the others, breaking fear's inertia and striding for the vestibule.

Calix beat her through the door and, with a flap of his coat, darted for his post at the entryway. El chased his heels, lighting a match and flanking the group. I set my incense alight, too, and took the final hall, unable to see even a body's length into its darkened reaches. The smell would draw the spirit to us instead of the others—or so we hoped—but we'd stand guard until they escaped onto the street. Only then would we double back and lead it to the altar.

The last of the tour group filed into the vestibule, packed like a flock herded out to pasture. Taran guarded the rear with the earnestness of a shepherd. I gave him my most reassuring smile—one he finally returned, as best he could, easing the knot in my chest.

I'd buy him a hot drink later tonight. We'd be fine.

Piri had the group almost past the fountain when the breeze picked up. A chill rattled the windows and flickered her gas lamp.

My body tensed, shoulders drawing up tight as a bowstring. I brandished my stick of incense with one hand, unsheathing my knife with the other, but nothing was there. Nothing, yet the fine hair on the back of my neck stood on end, and I could *sense* the heaviness in the air.

I wasn't the only one.

"Run!" El shouted, bolting from her post at the opposite hall.

Tourists scrambled for the exit as Ilia's wind whipped into a frenzy, guttering Piri's lamp and slapping one of the church doors shut. Yet, no smoky figure filled it. Calix turned on his heels, incense held high, eyes wide. But if it wasn't in El's hall, and it wasn't on the altar, and it wasn't at the exit—

Weighted air pressed upon my shoulders.

Oh *no.*

I backpedaled, knife raised. I'd checked every hall and entryway but failed to clear the one direction that mattered: up.

And from the rafters of the vestibule, a pair of empty, soulless eyes, stared into my own.

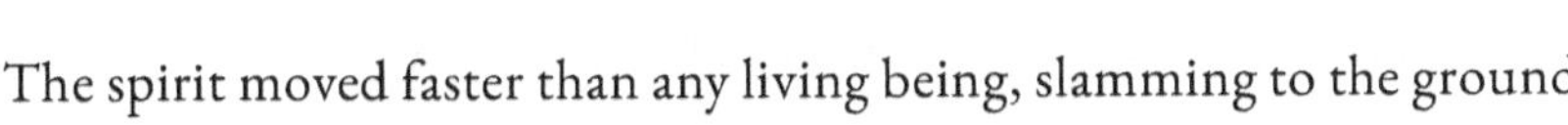

The spirit moved faster than any living being, slamming to the ground in front of the exit before I could shout a warning.

Piri scrambled backward. She tripped over her heels and landed, legs akimbo, beside the fountain. The group scattered, all but one doubling back the way we came.

Shit, shit, shit.

I drew my knife and leaped over Piri's prone body, charging to the center of the vestibule where a young, ruddy-cheeked woman stood. She froze, head tipped back and eyes wide, as the smoke enveloped her.

I was too late.

The spirit raked over her, crawling along her skin in a liquid slide. It smelled *wrong,* off, like food left too long in the larder. I dodged in, knife at the ready, prepared to cut it from her but unable to find an angle, for she fitted as she fell to her knees. It twisted away from my blade when she dropped, slithering across the floor in a column of oily smoke.

"Quick," Calix called. "We need to bar the doors—"

I wheeled around.

No. We wouldn't make it into the church proper before the spirit, and I had no illusions about what would happen if it trapped us in there.

"To the hall," I ordered, dragging Piri up by an arm to send her running.

Screams rang out from the front of the tour group when the spirit materialized in the entrance to the altar room, echoing through the vestibule. It filled the doorway from jamb to jamb, morphing into a menacing hulk with hunched shoulders and long-clawed fingers.

Great. A violent spirit with a flair for the dramatic: just what we needed.

"Follow me!" El called as a flame lit in the adjacent hallway. She'd commandeered a gas lamp and held it overhead, then turned and disappeared into the hall with coattails flapping.

The tour group turned, feet skidding over slick marble to follow her in a mad, desperate dash.

"Anya, is she . . . ?"

Taran crouched beside me and kneeled over the prone form of the northern woman.

I shook my head. "Get her under the arms. She might not be able to stand. Take her with the others—quickly."

For once in his life, Taran did as I asked. We boosted her up with an arm slung across his shoulders. Her chin dipped to her chest, eyes frozen open, body limp. Calix joined us, supporting her other side.

"Go," I said as the last of the tourists slipped into the hall on El's heels.

Calix opened his mouth to argue but appeared to think better of it, eyes flicking first to the altar doors where the spirit grew, then to the darkened archway past which the rest of the group had fled.

"On my count, Taran," he said, relenting and tightening his grip on the woman's waist. "One, two, three—"

They dashed for the archway. The spirit swung, fixing on them. A claw-shaped tendril snuck across the vestibule. I leaped in front of it, blocking Taran with my knife brandished, and it retracted with a hiss that raised gooseflesh along my arms.

Silver. I'd never met a supernatural being who liked it.

I had its attention and only a heartbeat to figure out what to do about it. I reacted without thought, throwing my knife in a hunts-man's shot that should have hit the spirit between its unnatural, empty eyes. *Should have*, because it disapparated before the blade struck true, vanishing in a cloud of putrid smoke. My useless knife clattered to the ground on the far side of the vestibule.

No time to retrieve it. I didn't know where the spirit had gone, but it'd be back to chase its quarry. What I needed was a distraction—one good enough to get the group to safety.

What a terrible night to have nothing but salt and a book of matches to my name.

Salt, matches, a brace of knives, and incense—the incense I still held. The spirit hated it enough to rage at its scent. Spirits weren't stupid, nor were they easily swayed from their course, but maybe its revulsion would buy me time.

I threw the stick through the door to the altar room, turned, and ran.

The hall was dark, with a distant glow at the end illuminating a line of scrambling northerners. My heels pounded in time with my heart. Up ahead, the light disappeared, hooking left.

El had found a bunker. I thanked the Saints by name, a whispered stream that bolstered my courage, even as the first cold lick of air brushed my back.

I sped, running faster. A cramp stitched up my ribs. No time to draw another knife. But safety drew closer, closer—

"Anya!"

A hand shot out, grabbing my arm and yanking me inside. The door slammed shut behind me. A crowd of bodies threw themselves against it—and just in time, for the moment its latch locked in place, an unholy bang rattled its hinges.

"Bar it. Here, grab this—"

I stumbled out of the way as a pair of northerners dragged a bulky object—a bookshelf?—past me to reinforce the door. They pushed it flush and held it there, backs braced against it, trembling as the hinges rattled a second time, then a third.

The bookshelf wouldn't be enough. Most spirits could phase through wood, fabric, and paper. Minerals in stone stopped them, though the longer they spent on this side of the veil, the stronger they became. Eventually, the church's stone walls wouldn't be enough, either, unless those walls were laced with silver.

That was where we'd gotten lucky, for this was no mere bookshelf. One of its glass-front panels was cracked, and the icons within had tarnished with age, but their shapes were unmistakable. The northerners must have thought the weight was enough to keep the spirit at bay. They were wrong but had unknowingly chosen the only thing that *could*.

The door rattled a final time, then stopped, leaving the room in heavy, empty silence.

I surveyed our surroundings, breath burning my throat. The tour group huddled in a wild-eyed, panting mass on the far side of the room, gathered beneath the flickering light of a single gas lamp.

A moth-eaten carpet lay underfoot, its original pattern lost to time. Relics sat upon the dusty cabinet shelves. An archway lay at the far wall, through which I spied the decrepit form of a collapsed cot.

We'd found the rectory.

"Yaya."

I spun.

Taran kneeled a pace beside me. The woman sat with him, back bent in a protective curl. At first, I thought she rubbed her arms, but as I leveled with her, I saw she scratched them instead, nails tearing into the fabric of her winter coat. Her wheaten hair hung on either side of her face, obscuring her from view. When I crawled around to find her eyes, I wished I hadn't. They stared at nothing, bugged open, unblinking. Her lips mouthed words, but no sound came out.

I'd seen what happened to the victims of spirits gone dark-side, but this was new, even for me.

The rush of the chase sapped from my shoulders, and I slumped to sit at Taran's side. Someone began praying aloud. The first sniffles of a child crying underscored his words. With it came Piri's voice. I turned to find her bringing some order to her charges, finding them seats, gentling the child.

Good kid.

"What do I do, Yaya?"

Taran's hands hovered over the woman's shoulders, not quite close enough to touch. Fear had melted his fury, but it was only a matter of time before it returned—and return it would when I admitted I didn't know what had just happened or what I was doing. I was a ghost hunter. And *that* thing wasn't a normal ghost.

The woman spared me the need to respond. She lifted her chin, hair falling away from her face, and croaked the first words she'd spoken aloud since the vestibule. They grated through cracked lips, a throaty tongue I didn't know. For a blessed, innocent moment, I wondered what north-ern dialect it was. Then I listened closer, heard the *intent* behind her speech, and my blood ran cold.

That was no common tongue.

I swung and found El beside the door. She shook her head, lips pressed thin.

Saints, what language was so archaic even a *spiritweaver* couldn't understand it?

I rolled to my feet, brushing off my knees. "What now?"

Jalti knew I had no idea. Between the two of us, El was always the one with a plan—not I.

El straightened, returning her attention to the barred door. Her hand rested on the edge of the cabinet, fingers tapping a rhythm along its decorative carvings. She took a breath. "Calix, you're on guard."

He took her place without comment, and she came to join me at the northern woman's side. The scrape of an unfamiliar tongue had quieted to murmurs, soft enough the rest of the group couldn't hear but plenty loud to keep a panicked line stamped into Taran's brow.

"Treat her like a patient," El said, dropping a hand onto Taran's shoulder and squeezing. "You're a gifted weaver, Taran. She's in good hands."

Taran's chin jutted out, resolve settling his features. He pressed his hands to the northern woman's shoulders and eased her to rest. I'd never watched my baby brother work and stared with unabashed curiosity until Calix rapped at my shoulder to redirect my attention.

"Try to pay attention, metalweaver."

"Do you talk to your doctors that way?" I swatted his hand, relishing in his flinch. "What do you want?"

Calix looked like he'd swallowed a plum pit but repeated himself for my benefit. "It's old, whatever it is. Older than any spirit I've encountered. The longer a spirit lives on this side of the veil—"

"The worse it is when they go dark, right. Now that we've stated the obvious, can we figure out what we're going to do about it?"

My words drew a whimper from behind me.

A young man in the tour group had eavesdropped and turned for his family, arms outflung. "We're going to die in here—"

El closed the distance between them, taking his hands in hers. "Come now. There's no need for that. I know this is frightening, and I've no intention to lie and tell you the spirit isn't dangerous. It's malignant—that much is certain. But there are three fine ghost hunters in this room, and I have more than one plan up my sleeve."

I knew what that meant, and I didn't like the sound of it. She had a familiar glint in her eyes, too—a glint that spelled trouble.

"What cockamamie thing are you about to do, Soti?"

She didn't turn to face me. No, she didn't look at any of us, gaze fixed instead on the cabinet standing between us and an ancient, malignant spirit.

"I'm going to go talk to it."

SIX

EL WAS ALIGHT WITH ideas. They cascaded from her lips, a torrent unleashing as enthusiasm set its hooks into her heart. It was hard not to get excited with her. She spoke loud enough for the group to hear her, and within moments, a circle of enthused, hopeful northerners surrounded her. Taran and Piri joined us, drawn to her side like spirits to summoning stones.

"It's an old tongue, one I don't know, but Ilia was a trade center in the early centuries. I can find one we have in common." El turned to Taran, reaching a hand his way. "How is she?"

Taran hesitated, scuffing the carpet with the toe of his boot. "Well enough. There's still something . . . off. But I settled her, and she's gone quiet and shut her eyes to rest. A specialist should be able to sort her out."

I turned to find the spot where he'd kneeled with the northern woman. She lay prone, face peacefully blank, with her head pillowed in a family member's lap. The strap around my rib cage loosened.

Attacks from malignant spirits took on a predictable pattern—an energetic interference with the mind. Healing the damage was beyond a metalweaver's abilities, but there were plenty of psychically inclined doctors at the university's hospital, so long as her symptoms progressed no further. When it happened in the field, most hunters knocked the patient out to stop the progression. But metalweavers had better tricks, and Taran didn't need a bludgeon to put her to sleep. Smart kid.

I patted him on the shoulder. "Well done."

"I didn't *do* anything. I just—"

"You're keeping her safe. No shame in admitting psychiatry is beyond you." I shrugged. "Old spirits can put a hurt on a head, and you're not a mindweaver. You did the right thing."

Wariness in his stance poked at my bruised ego, but he relented. "Thanks, Yaya." He turned to El. "What now?"

El sprang into another theory, words spinning faster than carriage wheels.

I let go of my misgivings, of the niggling voice in my head that fixated on the guttural rattling from the northern woman's throat, of the spirit's reaction to incense, of all the bits and pieces that didn't fit. I trusted El. She knew her business, and everyone in the room, hunter or not, could tell. After all, only three Ilian families claimed direct lineage with the Saints. The Sotis were one of them.

El's heritage was obvious when she spoke, for she lit the surrounding room. Powerful spiritweavers saw the world in ways others didn't. El had the gift of sharing that sight, and for a moment, I found hope through her eyes.

It was like no time had passed. If I pushed away the dusty corners and moldy relics of the church's inner chambers, I could snatch precious moments straight from memory and replay them. I used to stand with El on our hunts and watch her weave magic with her words. Though we worked with other teams, I was always the one on her right-hand side. I was the one she leaned on, laughed with, and broke bread with in our favorite cafe after a hard night in the old city.

If I shut my eyes tight enough, I could pretend we were back there again, could pretend El had never left.

I could pretend that I wasn't the only one who hadn't moved on.

"Anya?"

I snapped free from my reverie, face heating. I'd missed most of her speech, but hazarded a guess at what she'd planned.

"Where are you going to call it?"

"In the hall. It won't speak to me through the door. Not with this much silver between us."

It was exactly what I'd known—and feared—she would say. Trust El to call upon a malignant spirit, as if she were sending out invitations for a tea party. But what was I supposed to do, tell a spiritweaver no? I'd done it plenty when we worked together, but that was *before*, and this was *now*. I had an audience of thirty watching me stand toe-to-toe with one of Ilia's legendary Sotis.

Besides, she'd probably honed all manner of skills in the capital, skills I could only dream of watching in action. I wouldn't insult her with my misgivings.

As it turned out, I didn't need to.

"Talk is a waste of time," Calix said—rich words from another spiritweaver. "Didn't you see what happened back there? We need to banish it."

El pressed up onto her tiptoes, determination flattening the bow of her lips. "I won't banish it until I've tried everything else."

"You're mad. That spirit is dark-side—fully, irrevocably." He spun, turning his charm onto me with a flash of teeth and put-upon earnestness. "You saw it, metalweaver. You can't tell me you think it's redeemable."

I didn't disagree. Not entirely. But I'd be damned if I sided with a smarmy, two-bit clown over El.

"Are you trying to tell a Soti how to weave?"

The crowd hushed, and El went red to the roots of her hair.

Even those who didn't understand the first thing about spiritweaving still knew what it meant to be a Soti. El's mother ran the city council. Her older brother, Jael, was widely regarded as Ilia's most powerful working spiritweaver. He'd hunted with Silvershield for years. And that said nothing of their other siblings, or their cousins, or their aunts and uncles.

Ilia wouldn't even be a speck on a map without their family, and everyone in the rectory knew it—Calix included. As he did on the altar, he stepped aside, collar flipped up to hide the flush on his neck. I should have gotten satisfaction from it, but his hesitation needled me. El's words from the altar returned unbidden, *Unless you know something we don't*, and I repeated the same sentiment to see if it'd make him squirm.

"Well? Have you got something to say? Because you look like you're holding onto information."

Calix ran a hand through his flaxen coif, the tremor in his hands betraying his nerves. "Are you going to tell me that *thing* doesn't put you on your guard? Even after how it chased us through the hall? Even after *that*?"

I followed his outstretched arm to the prone form of the northern woman, chewing my lip.

Of course I was on my guard—what did he think I was, an idiot? We were stuck in a rectory with thirty civilians and nothing but a bookcase full of silver to protect us. I had no idea how to get us out of the situation short of a salt and burn, but that didn't matter. El had outsmarted a thousand impossible situations in the time I'd known her.

"Tell you what," I said, clapping his shoulder and turning away, "if this doesn't work, we'll try it your way next."

It came out a lot more gently than I'd intended.

Taran and Piri sprang into action behind me, moving the group to the far side of the rectory and arranging them in rows, while El and I put our backs to the cabinet. We shifted it only as far as we needed to open the door a crack—wide enough to slip through and not a hair more.

El went first, knife at the ready, casing the hall with the grace of an expert hunter. I watched her scent the air and drank in her profile, the flap of her coat, the perfection of her warding forms.

She was incredible. Why had I been so surprised when she went on to bigger and better things? Of course she did. Who in Jalti's name would want to get stuck *here*?

"Bet you're wishing you never came home for the holidays," I said as she finished inspecting the hall.

El huffed, eyes not quite raising to meet mine. A sliver of light from the rectory's lamp landed on her cheek. "Can't a girl get homesick?"

"Pssht. As if the capital isn't home enough—"

"Nothing wrong with being an Ilian hunter." El's tongue poked out of the corner of her mouth, brow furrowed. "I thought you'd understand that much. It's not as though you wanted to leave here when we had the chance."

I snorted. "When *we* had the chance. Right."

As if going along with her was an option.

El cocked her head, turning that light-eyed stare on me. I ignored it. Tagging along on a move to the capital would have hampered her and held her back. Plenty of weavers—our mothers among them—had made that abundantly clear when the offer came. It was addressed to *Eleira Soti* alone, with nary a mention of my name. Anything she said to the contrary was a platitude. She'd mean it, of course. El was kind like that. But it didn't make it true.

The capital wasn't an option for me. And asking her to stay? Even less fair. El had outgrown Ilia by the time we were in our early twenties. I didn't blame her for wanting to move on, especially when it meant establishing herself outside her mother's shadow. I didn't blame her, but it hurt anyway. Times grew lean when she left. El was the heart of our operation, and I knew better than to take on big jobs without the help of a spiritweaver. Hunting was my trade, and I was good at it, but there was a wide gulf between *good* and *good enough*. The way my contracts dried up in El's absence made that abundantly clear.

Beside me, El blew out a long breath and bounced onto her toes. "Ready?"

I drew both of my remaining knives. "Always."

The hall was a dark, empty ribbon, stretched taut in both directions. It took a minute for my eyes to adjust and find more than black, black, black in the distance. To my left, it continued in a series of archways, dead-ending a stone's throw from where we stood. A crumbling statuette beat its wings against the far wall. To my right, a hazy glow filtered in from the vestibule—a miniature smear of light.

The spirit was there, yet it wasn't. Its leaden, frigid presence didn't weigh upon my shoulders, yet my neck prickled.

"Is this close enough?" I whispered, checking the bare overhead archway, then swinging my focus from side to side before beginning the sweep again.

"It should be."

"Where is it?"

She rolled a shoulder. "Back in the vestibule. I think. I'm not sure. It's hard to get a read on this one."

No kidding.

I grunted, flipping my knives in my hands. "Can you hear it?"

The sliver of light from the doorway illuminated her face as she tipped it back, arms spread. Another spiritweaver might have been able to see what she was doing. All I could do was follow the beat of her heart, the thrum of her veins, the singing of each breath in and out.

El's body strained, shoulders drawn tight, limbs vibrating with energy. Cold air trickled through the hall—a breeze? The return of the spirit? I clutched my knives with sweat-slick palms and waited, but nothing came. Nothing and nothing—

And then the faintest whisper.

I startled, straining. "What was that?"

"You heard it?" El appeared at my side.

"Yeah. And if I did, it's not spirit talk, is it?"

We fell silent. El's throat clicked on an audible swallow. She heaved a breath, raised her hands, and tried again.

This time, the whisper came straight away—indecipherable at first, then louder, stronger. The words bled together, but I recognized them, for the guttural tongue was the same one that spilled from the northern woman's lips.

Beside me, El called and called, talking back in every dialect she knew. But the spirit didn't cease, repeating itself, a series of syllables drawn in a row. Sweat froze on my skin, pricking like a thousand tiny needles.

El shook her head and quieted. So did the spirit's whispers.

If it even *was* a spirit. The thought struck like lightning, sparking down my spine.

"Well?" I asked.

But El had nothing to say. Her cheeks lost their ruddy joy, brow wrinkled, fingers laced so tight the knuckles were white as bone. I shivered. If she was stymied, what hope did the rest of us have?

"That bad, huh?" I muttered. "Listen, what if—"

The door creaked. I whipped around, knives raised, to find Calix behind me.

"You tried your way. Now, let's try mine." He pulled a vial and a book of matches from his pocket. "Enough playing around. It's time to get rid of this thing."

SEVEN

I IGNORED CALIX, TURNING instead to El. She'd say her piece and get him to back off—I was sure of it. But El didn't move, staring up the hall to the vestibule with unfocused eyes.

A shiver trickled through me, and I rubbed my arms, leaning in to bump shoulders with her. "Tell him what you heard. You must have gotten something from it."

El shook her head. "This spirit doesn't talk. Not in a way I understand."

I'd never seen El wear the cracked mask of uncertainty before, and I didn't like it one bit. No way El Soti had bungled her weaving. She never failed. Yet, that brought me back to my niggling misgivings. El was sure she'd spoken to some long-dead Ilian ancestor—so sure she wouldn't entertain any other options. Had she missed the signs, or was I making clues out of chaos?

Calix muttered something and tucked the vial and matches into his pocket. He spun away from us and paced up the hall for the vestibule, coat flapping behind him.

I caught him in two strides. "Listen. I'm not sure this thing is what we think."

He pulled up short, regarding me down the bridge of his nose. "What are you on about?"

I ground my teeth. How to explain a hunch to a hunter who put no stock in my experience? I had nothing to support my claim but intuition.

"If it's a spirit, it's not a typical one. There's something *not right* about it. I don't want to walk in blind, and if El couldn't get through to it—"

"Seems like El Soti has lost her touch. What a shame."

He didn't sound sorry. My jaw twinged.

"I'm trying to tell you, one hunter to another, that something is off. If you'd stop being a prick for long enough to *listen*—"

"One hunter to another?" he scoffed. "Right."

Jalti, give me strength, or I'd offer him up as a sacrifice to whatever black-hearted thing lurked in the altar room. As if sensing my murderous intentions, El jogged up the hall to join us. When another pattering of feet followed her, I turned to find Taran on her heels, silhouetted by the light filtering out of the rectory.

Calix, in the meantime, had resumed his progress toward the vestibule. "Go back to the rectory, metalweaver. You'll be useful there."

Heat washed through my body. My nostrils flared.

"Turn around and say that to my face."

"*Saints*, you're a handful." He considered me over a shoulder. "No wonder your brother wanted me to come along tonight."

My vision darkened. I dimly registered Taran's "Anya, *don't*—" but heard nothing else over the banging drums in my ears. Two strides, and my hands wrapped around the lapels of Calix's coat, shoving him back to slam his shoulders into the stone wall. He was a head taller than me, and oh, watching the smirk fall from his face when he realized size was no object for a metalweaver of my skill was sweet indeed.

I could make bow ties from his guts—a fine idea. Not that I wanted to hurt him, not really, but I wasn't above making him squirm.

We froze there. He stared at me with eyes the size of silvermarks. Had he stopped breathing? If so, I was fairly sure it wasn't my fault. This time.

That's when I noticed the lump digging into my wrist.

Well, what do we have here?

The lump lay beneath the lapel of his coat, hidden in his breast pocket. He tried to squirm away the moment I let go, but I pinned him with a hand over his heart and a quick weave that locked his legs in place. Ah, yes, there it was—the satisfying flash of *horror* crossing his features as the metalweaver he'd denigrated stole his control.

I could only command blood for the iron it contained, and plenty pooled in a pair of legs. Not that bending it was a simple trick for the average weaver, but I'd come from a family of surgeons and had picked up a few useful tricks in medical school.

My lip curled. What would a spiritweaver know about *that*?

Calix's throat bobbed as I fished around in his pocket. I knew what he'd hid in there the moment I touched it, yet somehow, my anger didn't blossom until I held it in my palm. The multifaceted surface of a teardrop crystal stared back at me: a summoning stone. He'd used a thrice-damned *summoning stone.*

"You smarmy sonofabitch."

"Look," he said, holding up his hands, "it's nothing. The ghost might be a hair closer to the dark-side than I'd hoped, but it's still a spirit like all the others. We banish it. We collect the fee—"

"Oh, it's *we* now, is it?" I released my hold on him, and he stumbled, catching himself on the wall.

This was what I'd warned Taran about: a bottom-feeding ghost hunter who stirred up trouble, then demanded a fee for fixing the problems he caused. And the *precise* reason everyone hated second rates, beyond the general reputation they had as con men, was this. Every once in a while, one of them bit off more than they could chew, and people died to fix their mistakes.

Sure, I didn't have a ring contract—but I wasn't one of *them*.

"*We*," Calix repeated, straightening his lapels, "because the least you can do is pitch in with the salting after wasting so much time."

"I asked what you knew on the altar before we walked into that *trap*, and you said nothing. Tell me again who's wasting time?"

"Anya." Taran crept up to stand beside me, fussing with his cuffs. "What's going on?"

I held the stone out to catch the light from the rectory door. Prisms lit shafts of dusty air around us. "This is a summoning stone. An expensive one." I tossed it to the ground, spat on it, and smashed it beneath the heel of my boot, heedless of Calix's shouted protest. "Your 'backup' used it to antagonize the biggest baddie he could find. A stone with that fine a cut to it? He could have summoned *anything*. Do you even understand what that means? *Anything*. We'd better hope he actually knew how to use it, but something tells me we're not that lucky."

"Stop it with the histrionics. I know how to use a bleeding *stone*." For all his bluster, Calix kept his distance from me. Good. "And like I've been saying this whole time, all we need is a little salt and flame, and we'll be on our way."

I bared my teeth at him. "And how many zeros will be on the invoice you drop on Taran's desk tomorrow?"

"*Invoice*?" Taran gawped.

Wind blasted through the hall, stealing Calix's reply. It blistered, cold as frost, puffing our breath in clouds.

The spirit had returned.

My knives leaped into my hands, and I shouldered in front of Calix and Taran. The blades were as hard as they were sharp, and I crossed them with arms extended, warding the spirit away. It grated past us in a rush, unwilling or unable to punch through silver to get at us.

El charged ahead of it to the rectory door, which she slammed before it could slip in. Her quick-footed thinking drew a shriek in reply. The sound dug at my temples like the bit of a drill as the spirit ricocheted to the far end of the hall.

Calix took off after it. I charged on his heels, but I'd never catch him—he had legs like beanpoles.

"Wait," I called, "listen to me. We need to know what it is before we try to banish it." Even as I spoke, the spirit grew, encrusting the crumbling statue guarding the wing. "This thing is powerful. We have to work together."

But Calix pretended not to hear me. He lifted his vial and struck a long, thick match. The first words of a banishment ritual warred with the spirit's foreign tongue to win control of the hall.

Knives at the ready, I scrambled after him. I couldn't sheathe them to grab my book of matches. *Saints* willing, Calix's flame would be enough. Yet, instead of quieting and shrinking, the spirit grew larger, louder, extending until its edges spanned from wall to wall.

"Anya, what's happening?"

Taran. He'd followed me.

"Get back to the rectory," I said, not taking my eyes off the spirit.

Though he quaked in his boots, he didn't move. Unsurprising. We Iteris were known for our mule-headed ways.

El appeared at his other side. "It isn't responding. We need to—"

Calix flung an arc of salt from his vial to brush the spirit. It let out an inhuman noise, one that crawled inside my skull and sent me crumpling to the ground. I clapped my hands over my ears, pain ringing through my body and stealing my breath. I half expected to see blood on my palms when I pulled them away, but no, nothing.

El and Taran, too, had fallen at my side, faces twisted in grimaces, but were blessedly otherwise unharmed.

Then Calix's fire went out. I pushed to my hands and knees in time to register his scream.

The spirit had changed shape, shrinking into a dense whip of smoke. It wrapped around Calix's body like a toxic vine, holding him immobile. I scrambled for my knives—where were they? I'd dropped them when I fell—

There. One lay in front of me, mercifully within arm's reach. I grabbed it and staggered to my feet, swaying as though the spirit's primal cry had set something in my head askew.

"Calix," I shouted, voice cracking, "you have to run. Get your knife—"

But I was too late. Head thrown back, eyes wide, he was gone. The tendril of smoke dove in through his open mouth. His scream cut off. Silence battered at my ears. He faded, skin going pale, then blue, veins darkening, oily plumes curling from his nostrils.

Sweet mother of Jalti.

That was no ghost.

That was a *demon.*

Eight

Calix had used a powerful summoning stone and called for a malignant spirit. He'd gotten the malignant part right, but the rest?

"You idiot," I whispered, even as my vision blurred.

Ghost hunters were guardians and guides. We helped spirits cross and protected the benign from the ones that overstayed their welcome. Demons were another matter. They were ancient creatures, manifestations of evil, nothing like the ones we worked with, for they weren't human—never had been, never would be. But they used human bodies to suit their ends.

Calix was beyond saving. His limbs stiffened, then spasmed as the demon bore its way inside. Though it was too late to rescue him, I still had time to prevent him from becoming a demon's puppet.

I reared back and threw my knife. It hit true, catching him beneath his jaw.

The demon howled. Oily slick poured down Calix's neck, and smoke fled his body, shooting up the hall for the vestibule like a crossbow bolt.

Without the demon to hold him up, Calix collapsed, landing in a twisted mess at the statue's feet.

A shout rang from behind me. Taran darted past.

"Leave it be," I said, chasing after him. "We have to get to the rectory—"

Taran spun to face me, chest heaving. "You killed him. You're a metalweaver, and you killed him."

Metalweavers who became doctors swore to do others no harm. But I wasn't a doctor.

"No. Do you have any idea what that was?" I met his snarl-faced fury head-on. "That was a *Saintsforsaken* demon, one that caught Calix on his heels and fed off him to grow in strength. There's nothing left of him. He was dead the moment it got inside his body."

Taran's fists balled at his sides. His jaw tilted up, and he shook, fear feeding anger feeding fear. "You were the one who threw the knife."

I didn't have time for his righteousness. Not when he refused to understand the first thing about hunting.

"The silver drove the demon out of his body. Do you understand? The only thing more dangerous than a demonic spirit is one that takes corporeal form. As much of a dolt as he was, *no one* deserves to be a vessel of evil. I didn't kill him. I didn't save him. But I kept that *thing* from wearing him like a meat suit. Let's go before it does the same to us."

I tried to turn Taran away from the body, but he shook off my hand. "You're just leaving him there?" He backpedaled, then bolted, running for the end of the hall.

"You stubborn little shit," I hissed and sprinted after him.

Taran didn't listen. He never did. I knew what he saw when he looked at Calix's body: a dying man, not the already-dead. And, apparently, nothing I said was worth the weight of evidence his own eyes provided. If we got out of this alive, I'd strangle him later.

A flare of unwelcome pride lit my breast when Taran skidded to his knees and threw his hands onto the blackened wound in Calix's neck. Doctors did everything in their power to save lives. Whether it was wise to risk his own for a dying man, well—he and I could have a chat about triage after I was done strangling him.

I swung around to where El stood, hands clasped over her heart as though she'd taken a sucker punch. "I'll get him. You guard the rectory."

Her head bobbed, and she disappeared up the hall.

Now, I had to be quick. Calix might have sated the demon for a time, but it'd soon return for more.

I skidded to a stop at Taran's side, praying to Jalti he'd cooperate. Taran kneeled with eyes bugged and hand shaking. What little blood remained in Calix's body stained his skin dark. There was nothing else in that crumpled heap—nothing a metalweaver could save, for demons sucked bodies dry, feeding on life force and leaving behind a spiderweb of blackened veins. No wonder it evaded the strike of my silver knife. That much blood would have given it power aplenty with which to fight us.

"Anya"—Taran choked—"it's, he—"

"He's dead, and we'll join him if we don't get out of here. Do you ever listen to a thing I say, or do you think I'm so incompetent you'd rather become demon food than admit I know my business?"

Taran flinched. "I just. I've never seen anything like this before."

"Neither have I, and I'd hoped I never would." I pulled my knife from Calix's neck, wiped it on his coat, and sheathed it.

Normally, I'd leave it be—silver would keep the demon from returning to his body—but I didn't know where my other one had gotten to, and clearly, I was going to need it.

"That's—his body is . . ."

It was as though he lost the strength to summon whatever he'd meant to say, fingers curled uselessly around Calix's lapel.

The heartbreak on Taran's face cooled my anger. It shrank, lodging a lump in my throat. "Listen. Hunters train for years to fight things like this. It's not your trade, and I know you don't understand it, but *Saints*, Taran—you'd rather believe I killed a man? Just like that? What do you *think* of me?"

"He said—" Taran licked his lips. Even in the darkness of the hall, I spied the sheen in his eyes. "He said metalweavers were no good as hunters. That the best we could do was play along as a spiritweaver's helper. He's not the only one who says it. Mom—"

"Some twit you didn't know from Jalti came into your office, and you let him tag along because he told you I was incompetent. Is that it? And, surely, he must be worth his salt—or so you thought—because he said what you wanted to hear." I stood. "So, you hired a con who bungled a summons and saddled us with a demon, one I didn't bring the tools to fight."

"Anya, I—"

"Come on. I'll get his arms. You get his legs. Let's go."

A door slammed, spilling light from the rectory into the hall. El sprang into it, lit from behind like a halo. "Hurry," she said, "it's coming back."

"Scratch that—no time to take the body," I said, hauling Taran to his feet by the collar.

We took off, reaching the shaft of light as the first brush of ice prickled over my skin. I shoved Taran through ahead of me, bringing up the rear with El. The rectory was blinding, and I found handholds on the cabinet by feel to lodge it against the door. It skidded into place with a rattle and a thump and then everything went quiet. I collapsed, legs sliding out from under me, until I sat in a graceless slump.

"Well," I said, rubbing frustrated tears from my eyes, "that could have gone better."

Huddled with Piri on the far side of the room, the tour group kept to itself, but something about their demeanor had changed. A thick thread of fury underlined their mutterings.

Before I had the chance to tease out the reason for the change, El slid down the cabinet to sit next to me. "I told them the truth. They've earned it."

My sigh ruffled the flyaways hanging free over my forehead.

Taran regarded us one after the other, picking at his cuffs, then disappeared across the room to find Piri. I could call for him. I *should*. Discomfort had always riled him and sent him lashing out at convenient targets. It was worse when he was younger. He'd gotten better with age, but for all the ways he'd become a man in his time at the university, plenty more reminded me of the kid who used to crawl into my bed after one of his nightmares.

He was so much younger than me that I'd spent a lifetime letting him take unfair shots. I was the older sister. I wasn't supposed to rise to the bait. But, oh, I was sick of being his punching bag.

As if she read my thoughts, El wrapped an arm around me. The touch unraveled me, springing tears to my eyes. Sometimes, a fist was easier to take than a kiss.

I shouldn't give in, but I couldn't help myself. *Just for a minute*, I promised, and laid my head on her shoulder.

Calix was a fool, and I'd done the right thing when I threw the knife. I had no choice. But I hadn't become a hunter out of some misanthropic desire to spend more time with spirits than with people. Quite the opposite, really. For all I talked big and fantasized about having Calix's guts for garters, the reality was something else. Seeing him go out like that, being the one to put him out of his misery? It left an aching pit of nothing in the center of my chest. He didn't deserve to die.

I should have done something to stop it.

"What are we going to do?" El's whisper ruffled my hair. "It's a demon. I've never—Anya. How can we fight it?"

Her voice had that thick, throaty quality it took on when she stood on the verge of tears.

Tears?

I lifted my head, turning to face her. She was close enough that I could see them welling along her lash line.

Saints, that wasn't right. El was sunshine incarnate. She cried while playing with kittens or after a happy ending in the opera, but I'd only seen her like *this* twice. Once when her grandmother died.

And then again, when she left Ilia.

What in Jalti's name was I supposed to say? I had no talent with comforting words.

"You're the one who can talk to spirits. I'm just a metalweaver."

"*Just* a metalweaver? Anya, I thought it was a ghost the whole time. You say I can talk to them like it's some kind of cure-all, but it's not. I missed the clues, and now, a man is dead."

My head spun as though the church had turned upside down. "That wasn't a normal spirit, though, right? If it was, you'd have been able to reach it—"

Her lower lip trembled. "Spirits don't always talk to me. Usually because I'm doing something wrong—using the wrong language, maybe, or failing to connect. Weavers and spirits don't always get along."

I heard every word, yet none made a lick of sense.

"Are you beating yourself up because you didn't get on with a demon? I was under the impression they weren't great conversationalists."

A fat tear rolled down her cheek. I reached up to wipe it away out of instinct but froze with my hand halfway to her face.

"Plenty of spirits won't talk to me."

I blinked. "Huh?" El wouldn't meet my eyes. "What do you mean plenty won't talk to you? Did something happen in the capital? When we worked together—"

"Plenty of Ilian spirits went quiet on me, too."

My jaw flapped. El had *never* told me this, not in the years we spent hunting side by side, not ever. "I thought you always reached them. Even the stubborn ones. You're"—an incredulous laugh burbled out of my throat—"you're a *Soti*. That's why you always had the next step, the next plan—"

El grimaced. "Maybe that's what I wanted you to think—that I knew what came next." She hung her head. Another tear chased the first, running down the bridge of her nose to land in her lap. "I wanted to have it all together. We were young, and I wanted to impress you."

My heart tripped in my rib cage.

"How many?"

"How many wouldn't talk to me?" She rolled her shoulders. "I didn't keep count. Less than half but not by much. That's about what you can expect from a spiritweaver. Sotis aren't much different."

Saints, now *my* eyes stung. I should be furious with her, but it wouldn't take. If anyone understood what it was like to want the hunter they admired to notice them, it was me. When I first met El, I'd have given anything to get her to think I was impressive, and I'd done plenty of stupid things to earn her attention. Each of her compliments had lit me up like starshine.

Years of working together hadn't changed it, nor had years apart. El Soti was still the finest hunter I knew, whether or not the spirits always talked back.

I reached out a careful hand and laid it atop hers. "What did you do when you couldn't talk to them?"

She offered a pained, watery smile. "If spiritweaving fails, there's only one option left. Salt and burn. I don't like doing it, but it works."

"That's it?"

My voice climbed up an octave, drawing the attention of Taran's clients.

It couldn't be. When it came to salting and burning, El stepped back and let me take the lead. It was one of the few places metalweavers shone, and I had a knack for it, unsavory though it was. We'd had to resort to it so many times I'd lost count after our first high season. She always made the call to do it. I thought the decision came from something she'd heard or something the spirit said.

Turned out the opposite held true. El's decision was born from silence.

Another thought struck me then, even less comfortable than the last.

"Wait. I'm the one who taught you how to salt and burn."

El turned her hand beneath mine and laced our fingers, palm-to-palm. My heart skipped, face flushing, gaze falling to the bow of her lips.

"I know," she said. "I learned from the best."

I didn't have a chance to reply.

Taran returned from his conference with Piri, hands tangled in his cuffs, jaw firm with resolve. "All right. Calix is dead. There's a demon in the church, and we're trapped inside a rectory. How do we get out of here?"

I looked at El out of instinct. Her lips twisted in a self-deprecating smile, but she said nothing.

Right, then.

"I don't know," I said, "but if the years we spent hunting together taught me anything, Quicksilver Soti and I will figure something out."

Nine

Even demons fell for the old bait and switch—sometimes.

El and I separated the tour by age and strength, sending the fastest ahead with Taran and the rest in a second group lead by Piri. For all their misgivings, they were damn cooperative. It turned out fear was an excellent motivator.

The northern woman went with the second group. Her little sisters were a pair of tall, strapping twins who carried her with ease, cradled between their interlocked arms. I left them with strict instructions to get her to the institute as quickly as they could. Without Taran's intervention, she'd soon wake.

We charged up the hall, El and I in the lead, the drumming of scampering feet echoing behind us. Sure enough, our charge attracted the demon's attention, and the temperature dropped to freezing as we emerged into the vestibule. Its shadowy form filled the exit, as though daring us to make a run for it. Run, we did, but not to the street. El and I hooked a turn for the opposite corridor and took the rest of Taran's group with us.

The demon wouldn't have that, of course. It shot across the vestibule to follow, oozing along the ceiling as though to head us off. *Perfect.* Little did it know that only half of us had entered the hall. Piri's group would emerge to dash for the front door while we had it distracted.

I prayed they would make it, eyes on the oily slick of smoke pacing us. Darkness closed in. Shadows flickered along carven stone walls. The whole while, the demon followed, its grating whispers teasing ever closer. It was sure of its victory, but we had a little surprise up our sleeves.

We'd run for what felt like hours but must have been mere moments when I heard it—a shrill whistle echoing off stone. Piri had led her group to the street. *Thank the Saints.*

"Now!" Taran called.

We skidded to a stop. As one, our group brandished their shields: icons, frames, even a dusty chalice. The spirit billowed from the arched overheads, but hissed like a scalded cat when it touched silver and bolted past us to the end of the hall.

To their credit, the tour didn't need to be told to start running. They reversed course and followed Taran back the way we came. El and I paced one another, now guarding the rear of the group, limbs burning and lungs heaving.

I felt it the moment the demon realized what we'd done. My breath turned cloudy in the air in front of me, its rage sucking warmth from the hall. Dense, wicked cold crawled behind us, gaining with each passing second. The vestibule was a dim smear of light in the distance. We wouldn't reach it in time. The silver had startled it, but the little we'd scavenged from the rectory wouldn't be enough to hold against the full force of its strength.

"Pick a door, Taran, go!" I shouted.

At least, that way, we could go to ground and make another plan.

Taran hung a sharp right, leading the others through the nearest archway. Something plucked at my coat, and I flailed, slashing blindly behind me. But it was fast, and I was fleeing with my back to it. I'd have to stop and make a stand, which I wasn't prepared to do—

El grabbed my hand. Head tipped back, she didn't break stride as she wove, mouth open, eyes shut. Silver light glowed behind her eyelids. What in Jalti's name was she *doing*? If she couldn't speak to it—

An inhuman noise vibrated out of her—a deep ring, as if her chest were a bell, and she'd slammed a mallet into her rib cage. It was glorious, bizarre, a sound I'd never heard a body make. The demon didn't share my opinion. Wailing, it fell behind and lost its influence on the surrounding air. The hall warmed. We made it, following the last of the tour group beneath a carven archway. Once through, I turned and launched my knife, weaving out with my talent and shattering it into a thousand malleable pieces. It stuck to the archway in a spiderweb of silver thread.

Let the demon try to get through *that*.

I spun, catching El by the shoulders. "What did you do?"

Her laugh was the near-hysterical kind, one borne from a pounding heart and sudden relief.

"If spiritweavers can make sounds spirits love, we can also make sounds spirits hate."

She was lit up from the inside, cheeks aglow.

"They teach you that in the capital?"

"At least I learned *something* useful."

Beside us, the doorway darkened. Through the skeins of silver that had once been my knife, I caught sight of a pair of empty eyes. It shrieked a final time, doubling us over with our hands cupping our ears—retribution for whatever Saints-blessed sound El had made.

Then it disappeared.

"Well," I muttered, straightening the lapels of my coat, "I guess the capital's training is good for something."

Taran stepped up next to us, reaching out to trace the pattern of silver blocking off the doorway. He looked at me, then at El, mouth hanging open.

"You'll catch flies like that, you know," I said.

He ignored me. His fingertips followed a line that wound like the veins of a leaf from the center of the archway to its bottom corner. "This is. Wow." He broke off, lip caught between his teeth.

"She's one of the best," El said, chest puffed.

I rolled my eyes.

Let Taran work out what I'd done with my knife if he wanted—I had other matters on my mind. We'd ended up in an open-air courtyard. A central fountain filled with stagnant rainwater sat in the center of a flagstone patio. Ivy grew over the courtyard's walls. The tour group huddled around it where the moonlight laid a patch of silver, driving away the church's shadows.

I didn't know the layout of the church as well as an old-city guide, but this had to be its central courtyard. Three more darkened archways opened into it in cardinal directions. At least one of them would lead us straight back to the demon, and I had no idea which one was which.

"All right," I said, raising my voice so the group could hear me. "We don't have much time. One of these halls will lead outside. Another will probably double back and put us near the vestibule." I turned to El. "Thoughts?"

I expected her to take charge like always, but she didn't, hanging at the group's fringes.

"This isn't my territory. Taran knows the grounds best."

Taran turned from the remains of my knife, blowing out a sigh that ruffled his hair. "We never come this far into the church. I've seen plans of its layout, though, and I think I can pick the right tunnel. I just need a minute to orient myself."

"Take your time," a tourist said. "We don't have a demon on our tail or anything."

Taran ignored him. He paced the length of the courtyard, muttering and peering into one of the halls, then craned his neck to make out the shape of the stars in the patch of sky. I watched him work, but my attention drifted back to the doorway and the remains of my last knife.

"I wish he didn't look so surprised about it."

El followed my line of sight. "Family." She shrugged. "We love them, and they us, but sometimes, I suspect they have the least accurate perception of who we are and what we're good at."

I raised a brow at her.

"You know my mom," she said. "She wanted me to follow in her footsteps—to go to the capital and make my name there, then come back to Ilia and fill her position when she leaves the university. Maybe run for council someday."

"Doesn't sound like a bad life."

"No? Come on, Anya. You know how hard it is to live up to the bar set for you." I flinched. Her brow knit, and she reached out, fingertips snagging the sleeve of my coat. "Shh, I didn't mean it like that." Her face turned from mine. "I'm sorry if I was a part of what made that bar feel so high for you. That I let you think I had answers I didn't, answers that you would have had if you were a spiritweaver or a different kind of hunter. You had as much or more right to hunt in the capital as I did."

I huffed, pulling my sleeve from her grasp. Platitudes were the last thing I wanted.

But El wasn't done. She'd choked herself up, voice going funny.

"I should have told you how much I wanted you to come with me instead of trying to save my pride. I knew you'd say no if I asked, and I couldn't bear the thought of it, but I should have said something, anyway . . ."

"Why did you come back?"

El wouldn't look at me.

"Because I missed Ilia. Because I missed *you*. It's not so easy to find a good partner."

That was the truest thing I'd heard all night. "Well, if we're doing apologies—" I wrinkled my nose. I liked heartfelt conversations about as much as I liked getting punched in the mouth, but I forced the words out, anyway. "Maybe I should have asked you to stay. Or sent one of the ten thousand letters I wrote, asking you to come back."

Her head snapped up, eyes shining. "You wrote me?"

"Yeah, well, if you count a stack of unsent letters in my drawer as 'writing you,' sure." I scuffed my toe against the edge of a flagstone. "I'm sorry if—" Dammit, now *I* was tearing up, and I hated crying. "If I let you think it didn't matter to me when you left. Because it did."

She put me out of my misery, pulling me close and hugging me *tight*.

I buried my face in her collar. "I missed you so much."

El *vibrated* when she was happy, teary-eyed joy making her wiggle in her boots. "I left the capital for good, you know."

I pulled back. "What?"

"It wasn't worth it. Don't get me wrong—the contracts were challenging, and the pay was great. I was making a name for myself in my own right." Her hands warmed the small of my back, even through my coat. "But the hunters there are pompous asses. The ones who knew I was a Soti either hated me on sight or chased after me for a partnership. But none of them were *you*. And one day, when I was sitting down, getting ready to sign another winter contract, I started bawling my eyes out at the kitchen table. My roommate thought I'd cracked, but that wasn't it. I was ready to come home."

Saints, she was so earnest, and I heard the words she didn't say plain as the bell that had rang from her chest in the hall.

"Is that why you're here with Piri? You didn't come just to help her—you're in it for the marks, too."

She winced. "Moving is expensive, and it's impossible to get a contract in the middle of low season. I'd hoped to get by until the spring rush. I'm sorry I let you think otherwise."

"I understand." I did. It had to be tough to return from the capital and scrabble to make ends meet. Saints knew I was just as embarrassed by where I ended up after she left. Would I give her an earful for it later? Absolutely. Now, though, I had no intention of losing the second chance I never thought I'd get. "But you owe me a drink when we get out of here."

"Yaya," Taran called from across the courtyard, "I think I've got it."

El grinned at me. "Deal. If we're out of here fast enough, I bet our favorite tavern in central will still be open."

I threw an arm around her shoulders, and we faced Taran together.

TEN

"There's an exit down this hall," Taran said. "And if it's the right one, it should also branch off and loop to the vestibule."

That wasn't ideal. The demon might already lurk in the shadows there, waiting for us to make a break for it.

"Tricky," I muttered, patting my coat pockets.

"We could split up again?"

I shook my head. "Demons aren't mindless. It won't fall for the same thing twice, and besides, I'm all out of silver." I pulled a fistful of change out of my pocket to show him—not a silvermark in the lot.

"How were you going to get home?"

He sounded so much like our mother it stunned me, sometimes.

"Tips and goodwill, Taran," I said through grit teeth. "Neither of which we're likely to see when this is said and done."

A man was dead. A woman, injured. If we weren't quick about it, others would join them. The demon wanted hosts—bodies to feed on. It wouldn't go softly across the veil, no. Malignant spirits never did. We'd have a fight on our hands, even if I was properly equipped. As it stood, I was woefully unprepared to protect the last of Taran's tour group.

"We have to make a dash for it," El said, as if she read my thoughts.

"A dash, we can do," said a tourist, puffed up with far more confidence than I had.

At least he wasn't exaggerating.

Taran had split the groups with a keen eye for fitness, and the twelve who stayed had the hardy look of northern rural living—the sort who could run the length of Ilia's central district and hardly break a sweat. They'd test it now. We needed to get moving.

"Same as last time," I said. "Two lines. Keep your head on a swivel and your eyes on the two in front of you. It'll get dark in there, and we don't want you tripping each other."

They formed up, silence descending like a blanket of snowfall. A woman in the center of the column—the one who'd grabbed the chalice—handed it my way. I broke off the stem and gave the cup back. She needed the protection more than I did, and besides, a few passes of my hand sharpened the stem's lumpy surface into a passable point.

"It's too unbalanced to be all that useful," I said, showing it to El.

She slipped her hand into my free one and squeezed. Great. Now I had a lump in my throat to match the ones on my dagger.

"Ready?" I asked.

She pressed up on her tiptoes. "You take the front with Taran, all right? He'll need you. I'll take the rear. If need be, I'll distract it."

I didn't want to leave her, but letting Taran go alone was even less of an option.

"Be careful," I said. "No heroics."

Our shoulders bumped. El squeezed my knuckles tight, then let go and took her place at the rear of the group.

My heart thumped double time as I joined Taran.

He called for quiet and whispered a brief prayer to the Saints, hands caught up in the lining of his cuffs. Then he turned to me, a humorless smile on his lips. "Remember that thing you used to say about the monsters under my bed, Yaya? 'What's the worst that can happen? They eat you? You'll come back as a spirit and have the run of the old city.'"

Any other time, I'd have laughed. Trust a medical student to lean on gallows humor.

"That was a long time ago, baby brother. I've learned a few things since then."

"Let's hope so."

And with that, we were off.

This corridor was darker than the last. It passed in a midnight blur of panting breath and boots against stone. Taran lit his lamp when we forged beyond the moon's glow, casting ancient stone in a warmth I couldn't feel. He led us past a fork in the hall, one we didn't stop to examine, but lamplight let me see the satisfaction stamped into his features.

This was it. This was the way out.

The cold came slowly this time, a creeping chill seeping into my body almost before I knew it was there. It prickled along my spine as we turned a corner and found an empty archway a stone's throw away, lit by streetlights. *Safety*. It was so close I could taste it—but not close enough.

"It's back," Taran said, and we picked up speed.

Speed wasn't enough. Just as we reached the first brush of silver moonlight, a shout rose from the back of the tour group. A bell rang. The demon shrieked. I skidded to a stop, my shoulder pressed against stone.

Taran joined me, flattening himself against the wall and letting the group run past him to freedom. "Go," he called to them. "Faster. Don't stop until you hit the gate to the old city. See if you can reunite with the others. And send for help."

A match flared in the hall, illuminating El and the demon both for a hair-split second before the light went out. Then I smelled it. *Incense.*

"You want it?" El taunted. "Come and get it." And she disappeared up the fork in the hallway with a demon on her heels.

Behind me, the joyful cry of the tour group reaching freedom echoed up the hall. I should see them out of the old city. They weren't entirely safe until they passed its boundaries, but leaving El wasn't an option. My fist curled around my lumpy dagger. Could the demon double-back and follow them out of the church? I didn't want to find out it could the hard way.

The dagger flew from my fingertips, shattering into a hundred veins of silver in the doorway. Weaponless, again. It was worth it to buy the group time, but I wasn't the only one risking to help others get to safety.

I should have taken the whole damn chalice.

"Seal it back up after you're through," I said, spinning around. "I have to help El."

Taran's hand clamped on my shoulder. "You're not going alone."

I pushed past him. "El needs me—"

"And I'm not leaving you." He fell into step beside me.

Saints, when had my little brother grown up?

"You've seen what that demon can do."

"Which is *exactly* why I'm coming. Two metalweavers are better than one." He held the lamp overhead, highlighting the fork leading to the vestibule. "She went this way."

"And we need weapons. I'm out of silver again, Taran—oh, what, you *knew* that. Don't give me that constipated face—"

Taran drew a canvas bag out of his inner breast pocket and slapped it into my hand. It jingled.

It was filled with silvermarks.

"Payment from the tour group," he said. "My boss is going to kill me when he finds out, but I suppose if I die by his hands, it means we walked out of here alive."

I took back every uncharitable thought I'd ever had about him.

"Look at that, Taran Iteri the Renegade."

His pained smile turned a shade more genuine.

"Maybe I take after you more than I'd thought."

A scream stole my reply.

Taran and I froze for a heartbeat, meeting one another's wide-blown eyes, then broke into a sprint. This hall was longer than the last, winding toward the vestibule on a downward slant. I hadn't run this far in months. My legs weighed as much as iron sledges, and cramps stitched up my rib cage, but still, we forged onward—until Taran tripped.

He stumbled, arms flailing, gas lamp guttering wildly, and caught himself on a ledge cut into the corridor's wall. For a moment, I didn't register what I saw. It was a better moment than the one that came after, when I found myself staring straight into the dead eyes of a human skull.

I flailed backward. Taran whirled around, light swinging. He'd tripped over a bone—a long one, part of a leg from the skeleton I'd gotten up close with. It must have fallen from the ledge where the skeleton laid. The ledge? No, not a ledge but a rock-hewn burial bed. We were in a crypt.

It made more sense than I'd like to admit. I'd learned about the burial practices of bygone centuries in school but hadn't imagined I'd ever crawl around in the least savory part of a church. Believe it or not, even spirits found the doom and gloom of necropolises too much to manage in the afterlife. And the malignant ones? They wanted to be where the living were.

"We have to keep going," I said, not at all proud of the tremor in my voice.

This tunnel had to lead beneath the altar room. Even if it didn't give us access to the vestibule, it would bring us to El.

We took off again, Taran brandishing his lamp left and right. Dark pits opened in the walls on either side of us, piled with bones as though entire families were buried together. In some places, dusty approximations of clothing and leathery skin still clung to the bodies.

I winced. Taran was a medic and Jalti knew I wasn't squeamish, but this wasn't like the surgery. Dead of a different kind surrounded us, and my imagination galloped with every cobweb I ran through, picturing bony fingers stretching from tombs to reach my way.

That's when Taran went down again, his gas lamp landing on the ground and rolling. He flailed at the edge of the circle of light. "Get it off, get it off—"

I clutched the sack of silvermarks and dashed for him, breath held.

It wasn't cold. It couldn't be the demon, could it?

It wasn't. Whatever he'd tripped over this time had sent him shoulder-first into a tomb and brought a pile of bones down atop him. Swatting them away, I brushed the detritus of long-dead Ilians from his shoulders and helped him to his feet. Tremors ran through his frame. His breath came in shallow puffs.

"You're all right." I shook him by the shoulders, pulling from my repertoire of off-color humor. "And so what if they eat you? You'll come back as a spirit and have the run of the old city."

That brought a weak smile to his lips.

"Come on," I said, snatching the lantern light and prodding him up the hall. "She needs us."

We ran again, eyes ahead, watching our steps for any further surprises. The crypt wound toward the center of the church in a series of snaking turns. Just when I'd given up hope it would connect to the network of tunnels we'd already traversed, the passage widened. *There*, a flight of wide stone stairs. And slumped at the bottom of them, a body.

"El!"

I skidded to her side on my knees, turning her to lie face up. She was still, eyes shut, unmoving—

Ice. Behind us.

"You sonofabitch," I hissed.

Whipping around, I grabbed a fistful of marks and hurled them at the demon. They sharpened midair, splitting into a hail of needles, raking it with Saint-sanctified goodness just as it had raked the northern woman.

It let out a howl that vibrated the surrounding stone and made my ears ring, then retreated into the crypt's shadows. I reached into the bag and threw another handful. Before I could touch this lot, however, Taran wove. The tingle of his power raced along my limbs, familiar and unfamiliar, filling the crypt from end to end.

The coins burst one after another, turning to a spiderweb of silver, just as I'd done in the courtyard—a replica sealing off the hall.

He'd mimicked me.

The demon was a banshee of fury on the other side of the net. It raced away, retracing its steps. Was there another tunnel to the vestibule we didn't know about? Another way through the courtyard? Where *were* we?

I didn't know. It didn't matter. Nothing mattered more than the still form slumped beside me with a ragged wound in her side, blood seeping into her shirt.

ELEVEN

I PRESSED AGAINST THE wound in El's side. *Saints*, no. No, no, no.

"El." My voice cracked. "*El—*"

She didn't move. Didn't so much as flutter her lashes. I'd never seen her still like this, not even in sleep. Yet, she was whole, with blood in her body, blood that ran wet and warm against my palms. Had the demon raked her like that northern woman? How were we going to get her out before it returned for us?

My vision blurred.

"One of the best," El had said, but the 'best' didn't find themselves trapped in an old city church with a demon, unable to protect their family.

"I only just got you back," I whispered.

A pair of hands landed on mine, dwarfing them against El's side.

Taran. When had he gotten so big?

Our shoulders butted together. His head bowed in concentration, hair hanging into his eyes. "Her blood is moving."

The words didn't register at first. I stared at El's still face, her deathly pallor. Then I reached out with my talent, and, *yes*, there—Taran was right. Her heart struggled, but it beat.

El was alive.

Barely.

"I don't know what's wrong with her," Taran said, an edge of hysteria creeping into his voice. "The wound is superficial. It shouldn't be enough to do this to her, not so fast. I don't know anything about spirits, Anya. Help me—"

"It's blood poisoning." I chewed my lower lip, prying everything I could remember about demonic wounds from the jaws of my memory.

Though I'd never faced off with a demon myself, El and I used to assist with hunts gone wrong. As a metalweaver with medical training, I ended up tending the wounded more often than not. Once, during my apprenticeship, an elder metalweaver had me support a patient's blood flow, while they cleared the traces of demonic intervention.

That was the only time I'd ever seen blood poisoning healed, and it was no easy feat.

Shit.

I wiped a hand on my coat, then brought it up to cup the side of El's face. Her too-pale cheek was cool to the touch, eyelashes fanning over skin. We could try to get her out of the church and bring her to the university hospital. But blood poisoning progressed rapidly, and resuscitation grew more difficult with every passing minute. We didn't have enough time to get her to an experienced weaver.

Could I heal El myself? Maybe. A skilled weave would send her skipping out of the vestibule. But a bungled job would kill her.

Saints help me, but I imagined it—imagined knocking on Aluria Soti's door and telling her what happened to her daughter. Even if she took my word and didn't pin the night's disaster on me, even if she didn't think I was in league with Calix, Taran and I were done. He'd lose his spot at university. I'd never get another hunting job. Leaving for the capital wasn't an option, either. Ghost hunting networks were small, and word of mouth traveled fast. My name would be on everyone's lips from here to the coast in days.

But all of that selfish drivel was a way of ignoring the obvious, a way of preventing myself from seeing the thing staring me right in the face, the fear that made my hands shake and my throat seal tight.

El was dying. If I couldn't fix this, she'd leave me again—forever this time.

I traced the line of her cheekbone with my thumb. Her face blurred, but I didn't need to see her to *see* her, the fractal map of her veins, the iron moving through her blood in beat after sluggish beat.

"Anya," Taran whispered, "I've never studied this. I can heal the wound, but if that's not enough . . ."

I pulled my hand back, balling my fingers into a fist so tight my nails pressed crescents into my palm. If I was half as good as El thought I was, maybe I'd get to watch her open her eyes again. I'd get to listen to her harmless gloating, bragging about how she'd been right—that I'd lived up to the years of work and training we'd put in, even if it was hard for me to see it.

If she believed I was "one of the best," maybe I could, too.

"I'll do it," I said, "but I'm going to need your help. Keep her going. I'll draw out the poison."

Taran said nothing, eyes like moons, but he put his hands back onto her skin.

I tucked mine beneath her shirt, laying my palms over the wound. Her heartbeat picked up with Taran's intervention. The demon's essence wasn't difficult to find; it clung to El's veins like an oil slick, foul and slippery with eons of corruption. Extracting it was careful work, the sort of precision I hadn't mastered, even after years of trying. In med school, the professor of surgery nicknamed me "The Bludgeon." Never did that strike me as a truer nickname than now, when I kneeled with head bowed and El's blood on my hands, gingerly pulling poison from her body.

It ran thick and dark between my fingertips, oozing from the claw marks on her side. Taran dumped his last marks on the ground and used the canvas bag to sop it up, keeping it from sneaking back in again. I drew until my hands shook, until my body shivered with the effort and muscles jumped in my legs, threatening to collapse if I didn't take a hint and quit weaving. I couldn't. My work wasn't done, not until all of it was out.

Stars flashed in front of my eyes, vision narrowing. I melted into a slump, but my hands never left El's side. *Almost there.* The poison had thinned, leaving clean blood behind. If I kept my focus, if I stopped myself from growing inattentive and bumbling through the last of it the way I had in school—

Taran pushed my hands away. I tried to argue, but my gut flipped, and saliva flooded my mouth. The crypt spun in a lazy circle. At least I did El the grace of crawling away before upending the contents of my stomach.

"Let me finish, or I'll have to carry both of you out of here," he said.

I wiped my mouth with the back of my sleeve but didn't move. My arms trembled. If they gave out, I'd land face-first in what was left of my supper.

"You said you didn't study blood poisoning," I replied.

The inane protest formed with a tacky, acrid mouth. I'd pushed myself too far.

Or was it not far enough? El lay, unmoving, but when I tried to crawl her way, Taran nudged me back again.

"We Iteris learn fast," he said.

"Whatever you say, Osrin Aglaia."

Taran smiled at the name of our forbear—the sainted metalweaver who'd taught himself to heal blood poisoning and saved countless lives in the process. Then he rucked his sleeves, placed his hands on El's side, and picked up from where I left off.

My baby brother, future surgeon. If we ever made it out of here, our parents would be proud.

Color returned to El's cheeks as the remaining poison seeped from her side. I laid a hand over her heart. It beat a steady rhythm beneath my palm.

I regained my strength as Taran turned his attention to dressing El's wounds. He wiped the last of the poison from her side, then reached for the last of our coins. With them, he spun a fine mesh. They made a piece long and wide enough to cover and protect the claw marks. Silver would keep further demonic intervention out and prevent contamination, both from El's clothes and more mundane infections. The netting was flawless—as though he'd taken what I did with my knife and perfected it.

I squeezed Taran's shoulder. "That's good work."

He shrugged off his coat, tore a strip from the bottom, and wound it around El's waist to hold the netting in place. "I should say the same. I didn't know you could do that."

"There are a lot of things you don't know about me," I replied, though not unkindly.

Leftover dizziness from weaving faded. I wiped my hands dry again, leaving smears down the front of my coat. I'd worry about that later. For now, I had to find a way out for all of us.

"What next?" Taran asked.

I tucked a stray strand of hair behind El's ear. Her heartbeat grew stronger, breaths deepening. This was the closest call we'd ever had in all the time we'd worked together, and it was far too close for comfort.

"She'll need to have that looked at by a professional," I said. Bless him, Taran didn't take offense. "But to get her out of here, I'm going to need more weapons."

"The coin purse was all I had."

My eyes drifted upward to the dark hole where the staircase disappeared into the ceiling overhead. If my sense of direction was accurate, we were underneath the altars—steps away from the vestibule. But the demon would protect them with the full force of its power.

"We have the demon trapped between the courtyard and here. Where do those other tunnels lead? Can it get back to the altar through another pathway?"

Taran shrugged his coat back on. It hung comically high, frazzled ends barely touching his waist. "Maybe we shouldn't trust my recollection of the church's layout. I brought us to a *crypt*."

I snorted. "And after the way you squealed back there, I'm willing to bet you didn't do it on purpose." I ignored his scowl, shifting around to cradle El's shoulders. "All right. We don't have a choice—the only way out is up. I'll take her arms—"

"And I get her legs?" He'd already found purchase, tucking his hands beneath El's knees.

We stumbled up the stairs in a flurry of awkward limbs and riotous blasphemy. Years of living alongside trauma nurses had taught Taran turns of phrase that'd make a sailor blush, and we grunted our way up a story of crumbling steps and emerged into an alcove on the altar's wing. The grumbling was a distraction from the desperation of our situation—distraction that worked too well, because El startled us both when she drew in a sharp breath of waking.

"Quick," I said, "get her down."

We laid her on the worn carpet running up the center of the aisle, and I kneeled at her side to watch her open her eyes. She beamed when she saw me, teeth flashing, then winced, hand flying to her bandages.

"*Saints*," she whispered, adding another choice word under her breath, "that thing got me good, didn't it?"

Relief surged through me. I grabbed her hands, bringing them to my face, then kissed each knuckle. I absolutely wasn't crying. I *wasn't*. "You scared the snot out of us. If we ever get out of here, I'm never letting you out of my sight again."

El patted my cheek, an indulgent smile warring with the twist of discomfort in her features. "It caught me by surprise in the crypt. Well, I suppose the *crypt* caught me by surprise. I think I tripped over a femur—"

"*Ugh*," Taran muttered.

Her grin stretched impossibly wide.

"Aren't you training to be a doctor?" She pulled her hands from mine, prodding at her wounded side, a thoughtful frown carving lines into her brow. "Ah." The smile returned. "Seems I spoke too soon. Thank you, Taran." She turned the smile on me again. An unfair weapon. "And you, too."

I folded my arms. "Pfft. As if I could have left you down there. Your mother would skin me alive."

El tried to push herself up to her elbows but couldn't get any traction. I helped her sit, propping her against a dusty lectern.

"Where is it?" she asked. The smile fell from her face as we gave her the rundown. "So, you hit it with silver already—twice if you count when it was inside Calix. It's weakened from the hits, but it won't stay that way. If we go after it now—"

"*We*? You can't sit up. You're not going anywhere."

El rested her palm on my knee. "I know. But every moment we wait means a nastier fight when we face it. And you know what kind of damage a powerful demon can do."

I met her eyes, grim.

All those years getting called in as backup had set hooks in my mind. I didn't want to find out what this demon looked like at full power. Yet, facing it now was a terrible risk. El couldn't weave—not as injured as she was. I'd have to go in alone.

Could I banish a demon? An hour ago, I'd have scoffed at the very idea. How long had I called myself El's tagalong instead of her partner? I'd let so many hunters tell me I was a second-rate and never challenged them, not even when the kernel of pride I nursed inside my chest raged at their words. I'd let them say it over and over until I believed it, until I questioned my memory of those years I spent in contract as one of Ilia's up-and-coming talents.

As hard as it was to give myself the credit I was due, tonight had thrown one thing into sharp relief: I'd seen how a true second-rate operated. Spiritweavers said not to speak ill of the dead, but they hadn't spent the night cleaning up after Calix's mistakes. I had. In the process, I'd gotten the tour group out alive. Taran and I healed *blood poisoning*, for Jalti's sake. Now all that remained was a salt and burn. I'd been doing those since I was Taran's age. I could do it again.

I cracked my jaw. "All right. I'll banish it, even if I have to go alone."

"Not alone." Taran puffed his chest. "Tell me what you need me to do. Give me a pike, and I'll show it who descended from Jalti. But I won't leave you to face it without help."

His words rang inside my head. I looked up, fixing on the silver plating covering the altar.

Descendants of Jalti, indeed.

I squeezed El's hand. "A pike, you say? I have just the thing."

TWELVE

"I'm definitely getting fired," Taran muttered, rolling the silver plating we'd stripped from the altar's icons into a tight tube.

The metal went pliable beneath our hands, compacting into a hollow rod almost my height. Wide as a broom handle, it sharpened to a point on one side, wicked and thin like the pike Jalti once hurled from Ilia's rooftops to defend our city. The icons that made it were older than the Saints. Our finds from the rectory were trinkets by comparison, and Taran wasn't wrong to suspect we'd see retribution for defacing them.

But Jalti? She'd understand.

Once finished, we sat back on our heels and regarded our handiwork. Sculpture was our older sister's craft, and I thanked the Saints she wasn't here to point out every lopsided lump on its surface. This wasn't high art. It was a weapon, and for staking demons, it'd have to do.

I lit a match and ran it along the length of the spear, whispering incantations. Silver was already a holy metal, but I wasn't taking any chances.

"We have to go back through the crypt to find it," I said, face scrunching as I spoke. Picking my way through centuries-old bones was the last thing I wanted to do, but if the demon hadn't yet appeared in the altar, odds were we'd trapped it in the halls between the courtyard and crypt.

"Go," El said from her spot against the lectern. As if she sensed my misgivings, she added, "I'll be fine here."

"Fine or no, take this." I broke off another piece of silver from a nearby icon, ignoring Taran's wordless protest. Two passes of my hand sharpened a razor's edge along one side. Complain though Taran might, a weapon was a fair trade for the holy oil El had contributed to our cause. Turned out she was the only one who'd thought to bring it.

I handed the silver to her. "If it gets back in here, stick this in it and run. Or, well"—my eyes fell to her side—"hobble."

El's lips twitched. "Got it."

I brushed crypt dirt from my coat, suddenly unable to meet her eyes. "So. Any last words from a spiritweaver before we tangle with an ancient evil?"

"Don't get yourselves killed."

My own laughter surprised me, rattling in my throat. I moved without thinking, settling in front of her, fingers curling around the collar of her beaten-up coat. Her cheeks had regained their ruddy blush, eyes creasing at the corners.

I kissed her. Her lips were soft and chapped and tasted like her favorite winter spice tea. Flames raced over my skin, the first heat to touch me in hours. I pulled her close, cupped her face, and let myself imagine it all: a successful hunt, coming home with El at my side, stretching our legs out in front of the fire. Slipping her coat from her shoulders when the night grew long. Unbuttoning her high-necked collar. Loosening her hair from its braid until the waves curled against the small of her back.

Taran cleared his throat.

I pulled back. El's breath puffed against my lips, and I ran my thumb along the line of her jaw. "I hope there's more where that came from, Soti."

Her brow waggled. "I guess you'll have to come back and find out."

If that wasn't an incentive to banish a demon, I didn't know what was.

"*Anya.*"

I turned to find Taran shuffling from foot-to-foot in the altar's wings. Time to go. With one last brush of our lips, I stood, hefting my pike and meeting Taran at the stairs to the crypt.

"Already back with the ex, I see," he muttered, flushing something vicious, prompting me to turn a grin his way.

"Can you blame her? It's hard to resist the Iteri charm. I can give you some pointers later, if—"

"*Yaya.*"

My laugh cut short when we reached the bottom of the stairway. A nasty stain covered the stone floor where El had fallen. The remains of the coins Taran splattered through the hall stood intact, separating the entry to the altar from the rest of the crypt. Taran held up the gas lamp to investigate, but the far side was empty but for the bodies of the dead.

I blew out a breath. "All right." From my pocket, I extracted a pouch of salt and handed it to Taran. "It goes like this. We spray it with salt, then we pike it with silver. That'll lock it in its true form. After that, I'll hit it with holy oil and set it on fire. My hands will be full with the pike, so you're taking the salt. Even a few grains will do, but you have to make your mark." I looked him dead in the eye. "Do you understand? You have *one* job. Do. Not. Miss."

Taran took the pouch from me, clutching it like a lifeline. "I won't."

"Good. Let's go."

We peeled back a corner of the silver web blocking the hall, edged through, and sealed it behind us. If we'd trapped the demon, I certainly wouldn't risk leaving an avenue for it to get past us and come for El. Absent the frantic rush from before, the crypt appeared much larger than I remembered—larger and eerier, with a hundred hidden alcoves I hadn't noticed while sprinting to get to El's side.

"Where is it, do you think?" Taran whispered.

"I don't know."

A moment later, Taran stumbled, almost going to his knees. I swung the pike around to find the culprit lying innocuously on the floor behind us—the same displaced skeleton from one of the lower tombs.

"*Saints*," he said, "there're bones everywhere."

Any other day, I'd have ragged mercilessly on him for making such a phenomenally inane statement *inside a crypt*. But as it was, my heart beat so hard I suspected even Taran could hear it, a constant thump underscored by the shuffling of our feet, the creak of my leather coat, the far-off whistle of the wind through Ilia's streets. My guts were pudding by the time we reached the fork in the hall, finding it empty. Everything empty.

Taran chewed his lip. "Exit or courtyard?"

"Courtyard."

The demon would return to the doors. I was sure of it. It had a connection to the altar, and that's where it'd try to go. We'd sealed off one route. There could be others, though, and it would look for them.

We turned in silence. It took an eternity to retrace our steps to the courtyard. Instead of the desperate sprint we'd taken with the second half of the tour group, Taran and I kept gingerly with the shadows, pausing each time a creak of movement echoed over stone. Years passed before we sighted the faint glow of an archway around a distant bend. Yet, as soon as it came into view, the air in the hall dropped to freezing. Our breath misted. My eyes watered.

But this wasn't the cold from an exposed midwinter sky, no. This was something different.

"It's here," I whispered.

"Why isn't it coming at us?"

"It's waiting. It knows we can seal off the hall, but we won't be able to protect ourselves so easily in the open courtyard." I dropped a hand on his shoulder, squeezing. Taran's wan features flickered in the lamplight. "Listen. Whatever it throws at you, push through. Drop the lamp if you have to. We're only going to get one chance."

His throat bobbed. He nodded, and we turned for the doorway, striding through side by side—

To find Calix standing in the middle of the courtyard, face turned up to the sky.

THIRTEEN

Calix had his back to us, head turned so moonlight fell on a sliver of his profile. My blood ran cold. This was no miracle. The wound in his neck wept. Dark veins pulsed beneath his skin. He stood tall, yet he didn't, for this wasn't Calix, not anymore.

My guts writhed. I should have left the knife. I should have tried harder to get his body into the rectory. I should have—

My thoughts ground to a halt. *The rectory*. If the demon had returned there and recovered Calix's body, it had found another way into the hall. Had it reached the altar? No. We'd have heard El's call for help. But if we didn't stop it here, it would surely return to its favored grounds.

We had to banish it.

I shifted, brandishing my pike. Stone crunched beneath my boots and Calix—or, what *once was* Calix—swung around. Demonic essence oozed from his eyes, his nose, the corners of his mouth. It took all my willpower not to gag.

Taran grabbed my arm, fingers digging into my coat. The blood drained from his face.

"Listen to me," I said, pushing in front to block him from the demon's view, "that's not Calix. Do you hear me?"

He nodded but couldn't form words. The gas lamp guttered with his shaking hands.

That was the last thing I wanted, especially from someone who had to make an accurate throw.

"If you don't think you can hit the salt shot, give it to me right now."

At that, Taran found his voice. "I've got it. Now let's send this thing back to where it belongs."

Good. We'd show it what a pair of Iteri siblings could do.

The demon raised a necrotic arm, pointing our way.

"Scatter!" I shouted, pushing Taran in one direction while I took the other.

A blast of frigid air chased me, sucking the warmth from my body. I lashed out with my pike to cut the demon's power, but it was so cold the silver frosted, sticking to my hands. It seared my palms, and I gasped, regretting my choice immediately as ice tore a pathway through me.

I sliced the air again, taking a step, then another. Each pass of my pike interrupted whatever Saints-forsaken magic demons commanded, keeping it from freezing me from the inside out. I buried my nose and mouth in the collar of my coat and kept moving, kept pressing on. But not-Calix turned a chilling smile my way and raised his hand.

A wall of icy air pounded into my chest, sending me tumbling backward. I landed on my knees. The impact jarred my bones and set my teeth rattling. The only reason I didn't drop the pike was because I *couldn't*, and *Saints* did it hurt—like fire all over my hands. A thousand needles raked my skin. My eyes scraped against their lids.

I planted the base of the pike and used it to support my weight. One foot, then the other, each step agony on shaking legs. A gale whipped through the center of the courtyard, flapping not-Calix's coat around him. He stood within a blizzard of chaos, arms lifted to the sky, leaking eyes a seething pit. Moving toward him was like running into a storm. How could I get at him when I could barely walk? I didn't know, but I wouldn't let him win.

He wouldn't return to the altar. He wouldn't get at El—not while breath remained in my body.

The demon was so strong it bent the surrounding air, crushing my rib cage and nearly forcing me to my knees. Still, I pressed on, shoulders curved in against the blistering wind. My breath came in labored gasps. I held the pike in trembling hands, shuffling forward. Like a hunter. Always moving. Inexorable.

Each step I took sent it back one, then another, shying away from the pike's wicked tip even as it displayed the full flush of its power. One foot. Two. Three. I drove it where I wanted it, moving ever closer to the stagnant fountain in the center of the courtyard. Not-Calix must have known it was there but kept its eyes fixed on me.

Distracted at last.

This was my one chance. I didn't know where Taran was—couldn't turn my head to look for him. My hands locked on my pike. I steeled my will. I was a hunter. A metalweaver. My mother's daughter. El's partner.

With everything I had, I surged forward, leaping through air so cold I feared it'd flay my skin from my bones. It didn't stop me. I heaved my pike and drove it straight at not-Calix's chest.

It jerked away, darting backward, but when its stiffened legs hit the marbled edge of the fountain, it toppled in. That was the reprieve I needed. The cold air lifted, and I drew my first full breath in ages, a grateful gasp. I wound up again and stabbed at the demon but missed, pike clanging against marble and jarring the frozen bones in my hands.

It wasn't buried in not-Calix's chest, no, but for a hunter, this was close enough.

I smiled as not-Calix flailed toward the surface. "By the Saints of Ilia, let this water be blessed."

The water hissed and boiled as my incantation turned it sacred, Calix's body sacred along with it. The demon poured from his nostrils, a growing menace billowing above the fountain's slimy surface.

A flash of movement drew my attention. *Taran.* He charged across the courtyard to the other side of the fountain. Blood stained his lips, but he ran with all his might, the pouch of salt held high overhead like a war hammer.

"*Now*, Taran—"

He swung it like he'd been hunting all his life, hitting the demon in a shower of white. I pulled my pike from the water and hefted it again, joining silver with salt, before the demon could retreat. It wailed—a high-pitched noise, like metal scraping stone—and solidified, smoke recoiling and condensing. The trueform it revealed was the stuff of nightmares. Warped and fanged with pustules covering its oily skin, it swiped wicked claws at Taran's ankles. He dodged, and I drove in harder, pinning it to the ground. Its back-bent joints flailed, and it snarled, calling in its ancient, grating tongue.

Taran's hands joined mine on the pike, his teeth grit. "Do it, Anya. Quick."

I ripped my skin from still-frozen metal, and oh, it was blinding-white pain, but I had no time to process it. I smashed the vial of holy oil open on the edge of the fountain and poured it on the demon's trueform. It thrashed, screaming a curse upon our family, I'm sure, but it was too late. We'd trapped it on a pike like the one Jalti threw centuries ago.

The match crackled when I struck it, flame sparking between my fingertips.

Spiritweavers warned against meeting a demon's eyes, but they could take their superstitions and stuff them. I wanted this thing, this creature, this *killer*, to look me right in the face as I banished it across the veil, never to return.

The deep-set eyes of its trueform burned like coals. It had no place here.

"Begone, beast," I said, first in Ilian, then in the ancient tongue of those who came before. "Our city isn't yours. It never will be."

The demon screamed.

I dropped the match, and it burst into flames.

Taran and I sprang back, hands over our ears in a futile attempt to block out its howling.

Flames enveloped its body, cracking its skin, racing through its veins and blistering its bones—

And then, just like that, it winked out of existence, sucked through the veil to whatever hell it had crawled out of.

The pike fell with a clang.

I blew out a slow breath, limping to the fountain. My hands were wrecked, but they'd heal. I still had work to do.

Calix's waterlogged body was heavier than an altar full of silver, but I managed to drag it out of the fountain by the armpits to lay it on the stony ground. I snapped a piece from the end of the pike to set beneath his tongue. We owed him more than that, but it was all I had.

"I'm sorry," I whispered and shut his eyes with my fingertips.

I pushed myself to my feet with a groan. Was this why old hunters complained about their knees? Mine felt like they'd been beaten with an ice pick. I found Taran standing beside my fallen pike, staring at the place the demon had been.

"You look like one of those snakes that unhinges its jaw to eat."

My voice was rusty, throat sore. My mouth tasted of iron.

A near-hysterical laugh burbled out of his throat. He scrubbed a hand down his face. "Saints, when Mom hears about this—"

I groaned. "No, please don't." I winced as I put weight on my ankle. Apparently, I'd wrenched it during the fight. Great. "Come on. We need to get to El, and I'm not going through that crypt again."

Taran caught me in a stride. He was worse for the wear, too, ragged and puffing with effort as we pulled the remains of my knife from the doorway and headed for the vestibule. Our gas lamp had smashed during the banishing, so we made our way in the dark, lighting matches to parse which direction to take each time the hall came to a turn. There was too much to say. Everything to say. So, naturally, we shuffled the entire way in painstaking silence.

We'd made it to the vestibule before Taran broke it.

"Anya." He chewed his lower lip. "Look, I—I'm really, really sorry."

"Pfft." I turned away.

"No, I mean it." He caught me by the elbow, spinning me to face him. "I brought Calix. I let him talk me into this."

"You didn't know any better."

"Because I didn't listen. Isn't that what you always say?" His lips gave a wry twist. "I didn't understand what hunters did."

Sighing, I ruffled his hair. "No, but I understand what it's like growing up in our family. I went to medical school. I know how Mom and Dad are. And if Mom said half the things to you she did to me, you've spent your life thinking there was only one way to get it right. A single step in the wrong direction, and everything—all those years of school, all your effort, all your little successes—went to waste. Ghost hunting doesn't fit into that story so well, does it?"

"Now it does." My surprise must have shown on my face because he continued with the same earnest passion he once used to convince me to quit hunting and take another shot at becoming a medic. "I study at university because I want to help people. You hunt for the same reason, don't you? If the rest of the family can't see that, I understand why you left."

When he put it like that, he made me sound soft inside. He was right. I hated it.

"Yeah, well. If I'd known how much leaving would hurt you, maybe I'd have stayed, anyway."

"I think I'm glad you didn't."

I socked him in the shoulder in mock offense. "*Ouch*, kid—"

"No, Yaya, listen. You'd have been miserable, right? And you're good at this, you know. Really good."

He was going to make me tear up again, looking at me with those little-kid eyes that used to con me into telling him way too many bedtime stories.

"Well. You're the first one in our family to admit it, so you're forgiven, all right?" His smile turned so bright I had to look away, scuffing my boots over marble tile. "Hey, why don't you come over after your shift next week? We can have ourselves a nice sampling of street food, a few glasses of spice wine, play a round of marbles . . . like old times—but with liquor."

Taran snorted. "Optimistic, are we?" Before the dismissal sank in, he added, "You say that like I'll still have a job next week."

"Ah, well," I said, heading for the altar room doors with a spring in my step, "there's always hunting."

Fourteen

I DIDN'T GET THREE steps inside when a body barreled out of nowhere, slamming into me like a short, compact dart.

"I knew it!" El cried, throwing her arms around my neck.

"You scared the skin off of me," I said, not proud of how shaky I sounded. My heart pounded. I may have squealed. Possibly. "What are you doing up? You should be resting—"

El grabbed me by the shoulders and spun us in the church aisle. "I heard its death throes from here. What happened? Where did you find it? Tell me *everything*."

I shouldn't have indulged her so easily, but Taran was all-too-eager to tell the story of the banishment, bouncing like a puppy let off the leash. Their excitement was contagious, and I let myself lean into it, washing away the lingering freeze of the demon's attacks. Taran sobered when he spoke of what became of Calix. We made the sign of the Saints over our hearts, wishing him a speedy journey. Even I didn't hold grudges against the dead.

"Demonic possession," El said, shaking me by the shoulders. "The last time a hunter exorcised and banished one without losing half their team was—"

"When we were in school. I know, I know."

El bounced on her tiptoes, eyes alight. "Do you? Anya, everyone in the city will be knocking down your door. You'll get calls from all the rings—"

"*We'll* get calls—"

"They might even let us into Silvershield, Anya. This is amazing. *You're* amazing."

"I had help." I ruffled Taran's hair again, delighting in his indignant squawk. "Now, come on, let's get out of here. This place is giving me the shivers."

I tucked an arm around El's waist and listened to the rest of Taran's joyful chatter, slaking her thirst for details. Victory buoyed us into the vestibule, past the fountain, and to the door where the northern woman had fallen. We limped together, a trio of walking wounded. And for the first time in a long time, I remembered how much I loved being part of a team. How much I'd missed it.

But I had little time to bask in it. When we pushed through the doors to the moonlit Ilian night, we found a swarming crowd in the street. Our tour group huddled in the shelter of a crumbling building across the way. They turned and cheered when they saw us, drawing the attention of a team of medics, and—oh. Senior spiritweavers, freshly dragged from the university in their midnight-blue robes. Several teams of hunters flagged them, all wearing the emblems of the city's biggest rings. A gaggle of passersby from the central district crowded the edges. I recognized a handful of reporters walking among them.

"We're never going to hear the end of this," I muttered.

El rested her head on my shoulder. "No, probably not." She buried her nose in my neck and laughed, sending a shower of warm tingles down my spine.

"I'll send for a carriage," Taran said. He wrung his hands in his cuffs, then disappeared down the steps.

Bless him. He *also* headed off a senior spiritweaver, who stalked across the churchyard with a thundercloud on her brow. I guided El to sit with me on a stone balustrade, tucking her into my side. At the far end of the street, the medics had started their approach. That was for the best. My hands were killing me.

"So, what now?"

El's breath puffed over my skin. "Now, I think I'm about to get more stitches in my side than I ever wanted."

"And after that? Where are you staying?" My brows shot up at her grimace. "Seriously? With your family? Aren't you going nuts?"

She lifted her head from my shoulder, nose wrinkling. "Why do you think I volunteered to join Piri on the tour? Marks, sure, but *anything* to get out of the house."

Hesitating, I scanned her features as though I'd find assurance or answers there. El was gorgeous. Moonlight fell on her just so, turning her eyes more silver than blue. I wanted to kiss the bow of her lips, the graceful column of her neck, the dip between her collarbone. I wanted to relearn every inch of her. To wake up with the silky slip of her hair fanned out across my pillow. To make an attempt at breakfast and utterly ruin her order of eggs, then argue about whose turn it was to do the dishes.

"Well. They'll probably keep you overnight to watch for infection. A few days, even. But when you're out"—I reached into my coat pocket and extracted my key, then slipped it into El's palm and curled her fingers around it—"you could stay with me for a while. Just until you get on your

feet. Or not. If you'd rather—look. No obligation, okay? No hurry. I—"
Shit, I was bungling it, wasn't I? "I want to do this right."

El stared at the brass in her palm. "How are you going to get home?"

"I have a spare."

I could break into my apartment later. It'd be worth it.

"Is this a promise?"

"What promise?"

"That we're going to give this another try? Just like old times?"

My usual bluster deserted me, leaving nothing but saccharine earnestness behind. Was this where Taran got it from? For his sake, I hoped not.

"Like old times but better. And I, uh—" I swallowed. "There are some
things I want to do differently this time around."

El's smile was so bright I swore it lit the entire street, bringing sunshine
to Ilia on a windy, midwinter night.

I kissed her.

The medics, of course, interrupted us, with Taran chasing their heels.
He'd arranged for a carriage with a young metalweaver in the driver's seat.
I cringed.

Poor El—this would be a bumpy ride.

"Weaver Soti, a pleasure," one medic said, making the sign of the Saints
over her heart. Her eyes flicked to me, brow wrinkling.

She clearly had no idea who I was.

That was fine.

"Anya." Taran chewed his lip, hands making mince of his cuffs. "I talked
to one of the senior spiritweavers. I told them you'd want to see El to
the doctor, but they're insisting on interviewing you. I don't know what
happened with the demon at the end, exactly, but apparently, it was bad
enough that every spiritweaver in the city heard its call."

I snorted. "No kidding."

El brushed a kiss against my cheek. "Go on, then," she said, standing with the medic's help. She pocketed my key. "I'll be fine. And I'll see you when I'm out?"

"I'll come visit as soon as I can."

I stood back while the medics helped her into the carriage, who were already poking and prodding her with instruments. She accepted it all with her usual smile, chatting with one of the junior metalweavers who preened at her compliments.

El waved out the window as the carriage sprang into motion. But her eyes skipped from mine to something behind me, and the smile fell from her face.

"Sorry, love," she mouthed. Then the carriage turned a corner and disappeared out of sight.

What?

"Anya Iteri, I should have known you'd be involved with this."

Oh no.

I spun to find a blue-robed woman stalking my way, face like a storm cloud, gray braid swinging behind her. Aluria Soti. El's mother.

"What's this I hear about a demonic spirit?" she demanded.

I sighed, and my disaster of a night grew a little longer.

FIFTEEN

"IF YOU DON'T HURRY, we're going to be late," I called, thumbing through a stack of correspondence with my heels kicked up on our table.

We had piles of unsorted mail covering most available surfaces in the apartment, all proposing contracts or seeking help with wayward spirits. No matter how many I had read, though, I never grew tired of seeing my name printed beside El's.

Not *Eleira Soti and metalweaver*—not anymore.

Anya Iteri and Eleira Soti, Silvershield.

Our names sat atop our new address—an apartment two floors above my old one. It wasn't much, but it was *ours*, with a brazier to warm it in the winter and a heartwoven rug gifted to us as a house-warming present by one of my sister's friends from the art institute. It was woven with a blessing—or so my sister had said—to conjure beautiful images out of its owner's head and display them in moving, living color across the rug's surface.

Unfortunately, the rug had decided its owner was neither El nor I, attaching instead to our new kitten, Mister Fluff. As it turned out, Fluff dreamed incessantly of pigeons.

Said pigeons flitted across the rug beneath my back-bent chair legs, flapping from edge to edge in a loop. At least the rug interpreted them with grace, putting vibrant colors in their wings to resemble the birds roosting outside our window in only the vaguest way.

"El, come *on*—"

She appeared in the doorway to our bedroom, shirt riding up her stomach as she reached behind her head to start her braid.

Loose maple strands cascaded over her shoulders to tickle at her belt. Her teeth worried at her lower lip, a line of focus furrowing her brow. Spring's brighter days dappled freckles across her nose. *Saints*, she was gorgeous.

I stood, sending my chair skidding across the rug, and crossed our modest living room in two strides. She smiled up at me when I reached her, tilting her head for a kiss. I obliged, of course, and slipped my hands around her waist, tracing the line of enticing bare skin at her waistband.

El squeaked, dancing backward away from me. "Don't you *dare*, Iteri. The last time you looked at me like that we were *two hours* late, and you're the one complaining about timeliness—"

I grinned, catching her again and planting another kiss on her lips before releasing her to finish her braid. My coat hung on a hook by the door, and I slipped it on, taking inventory of everything we'd need for the evening's hunt. Incense, matches, salt, oil, knives—all where they ought to be.

This shouldn't be a difficult one, but I'd learned my lesson and came prepared for the worst every time. A glance out the window confirmed our carriage had arrived. The driver was Taran's age, perched with legs dangling out the driver's side, a book in hand.

"Ready?" I asked.

El pulled her coat from its hook and joined me in the hall. We thundered down two flights of stairs to my old door, banging until it rattled on its hinges. It opened a crack, revealing Taran's wary face.

"Come on, twerp, we're going hunting," I said.

Taran rolled his eyes. "Anya, I'm studying."

As if that was a real excuse. He was already dressed for a night in the old city, wearing a secondhand coat he'd bought with the money awarded to us by the institute for banishing the demon. The prize had lasted him the better part of the winter, but he'd started taking jobs with us anyway, hoping to scrounge up marks after decidedly losing his tour guiding job.

Mom hadn't been pleased, but she'd let him move into my old apartment. She even surprised me by giving her blessing for Taran to learn my business—so long as he swore not to drop out like I did.

It was a fine truce, really. Taran was a good hunter, but he'd be an even better surgeon. I'd skin him if he so much as considered leaving university.

Until he graduated, though, we could have some *fun*.

"All right," he relented, tossing his textbook onto the table and shoving a pouch of silvermarks into his pocket. "Where to, this time?"

I grinned. "Ever seen a poltergeist?"

Color drained from his face.

"Yaya, *no*—"

El and I grabbed his arms and dragged him from his apartment, shutting the door behind us. We pulled him through the hall, down the stairs, and out into early evening twilight, where the carriage driver waited.

"To the old city gates," I said, hopping into my seat, "and try not to kill us on the way there, okay?"

El grinned at me over Taran's head. "Just like old times." She reached behind Taran's shoulders to lace her fingers with mine.

I gave her hand a squeeze. "Like old times but better."

The carriage jolted into motion, taking us down the street and off into the darkening Ilian night.

Join the Crew!

Thank you for giving this spooky little novella a chance, and I hope you enjoyed reading it as much as I enjoyed writing it!

That said, the best part of writing is getting to build a relationship with *you*. And wherever you're active, there's a good chance I'm there.

If you're looking for updates, ARCs, sneak peeks, and (monthly) writing tips, check out my newsletter. Subscribers get first notice—and first dibs—when I have new work coming out.

Can't wait until work hits the press? You might like my Patreon, where I post rough drafts as I write them. Patrons also get a look at my short stories, "writer beware" industry news, monthly craft of writing blogs, and patron-exclusive channels within my discord server.

Interested in following me on social media? I'm on all the apps @ceemtaylor, or you can find me on my website: cameronmontaguetaylor.com .

—◦—

You can make a difference!

Reviews are a big part of how I get my stories into the hands of readers who enjoy them. If you'd like to support an indie author, please consider leaving an honest review on your retailer website, Goodreads, or even social media—it really makes a difference!

Pirate by day and writer by night, Cameron "Cee" Taylor is a tallship sailor, developmental editor, and author of fantasy novels with thick romantic threads. Cee is most easily summoned with promises of kittens and freshly brewed coffee, but otherwise, you can leave a message @ceemtaylor on all the apps or grab a direct line at cameronmontaguetaylor.com.

Acknowledgments

There's a never-ending list of thank yous to put out into the universe, but let's start with Dan for forever and always having faith in me and my writing. Thank you for helping me find the courage to share my work with the world.

To Kerry, for listening to many, many cumulative hours of rambling about my maladaptive daydreams (and for always being a woon).

To Dad, for all those ad lib bedtime stories about ninja turtles summiting volcanoes, and to Mom, for always encouraging me to write . . . even when I was too tiny to put words to paper without your help.

To August, Alistair, Sio, and Monica for *literally everything*: critique partnering, emotional support, late-night-worldbuilding shenanigans, coffee shop writing sprints, talking me off the ledge, and insisting I never talk smack about my spooky little novella, even when I was *very* sick of looking at it.

To Chucks (and also: Charles). I'm ever-grateful that I've found my writing community.

To Susan, Hannah, Holly, and Rosedale: your support has literally been life-changing. Thank you.

To my EBC baddies for, day-in and day-out, making me feel less alone.

To Mr. G, for always keeping my mousepad warm.

And of course, to Samantha Pico of Miss Eloquent Edits for sharpening my prose, insisting that *no Cee, commas are not just a "vibe,"* and all-around preventing me from showing my ass to the internet.